MW01116099

SWEATY COLOGNE

SHAUNN NORTHERN

This project was created in consideration of every human being
who can still find it useful to give a fuck...

To the Review Board at The University of Chicago Hospital for Mental Health, Hyde Park Campus, the Circuit Courts of Cook County, Dr. Julissa Irving, PsyD, and to anyone who may have stumbled upon this writing by chance,

My name is Walter Mosley, patient #3324D, and I am requesting that the following arrangement be used in justification of my petition for discharge under the Mental Health and Developmental Disabilities Code of Illinois:

I, Walter Mosley, declare that the following statements are an accurate account of my experiences, to the best of my memory and belief. I, Walter Mosley, am fully aware that these words may be presented as evidence in a court of law and I am prepared to accept the consequences of perjury if any part of this document is found to be false or misleading.

With this declaration, I humbly petition for a thorough reevaluation of my mental health status. I seek the opportunity for a full hearing, presided over by a qualified judge, jury, and a team of skilled mental health professionals. My aim is to establish my eligibility for release and return to society, where I aspire to live as a free human being.

As I pen these words, the weight of institutional confinement bears down on my soul. The stark reality of my situation compels me to speak boldly and plainly about my experiences. What follows is deeply personal and only meant for serious eyes that can keep an open mind to the truth of my circumstances and the validity of this heartfelt petition.

For five long years, I've been trapped inside the dirty-ass walls of the University of Chicago Hospital for Mental Health.

That's 63 months. 1,916 copies of the same damned day...

Every night, I fall asleep to the sound of a madman's maniacal laughter. Each morning, I wake to the sound of my neighbor, Rooster —a grown-ass man who likes to crow at the sun. The air in here is stale, like the wind has never made it indoors. Harsh fluorescent lights often flicker and buzz. Worse of all, in the depths of this madness, I can hear patient #3235A's loud sadness, moaning, wailing, and crying at once, like an injured deer left bleeding on the side of a road. His cries seep through the walls and straight to my heart.

I move through my days like a ghost—eating in silence, faking my pills, then back to my room where I can keep to myself. Like clockwork. It's a grim routine, as predictable as it is soul-crushing.

Dr. Julissa Irving, my assigned therapist. Despite my attempts to convey the truth of my experiences, she dismisses my stories as delusions, my family history as fantasy. In her clinical opinion, I'm nothing more than a textbook case of undifferentiated schizophrenia. She asserts, with unwavering certainty, that there's no such thing as family curses. Thinks I made it all up. Says my brain and nervous system are broken.

But I know the truth, and I'm done giving a damn about the opinions of ignorant fools who think I'm crazy. I finally understand who I am, what I'm made of, and what I've seen with my very own eyes. So, as you delve into my story, I implore you to approach it with an open mind and heart. I am not schizophrenic. I am not a bully. I am not a heartless killer. I am not the man you see at the surface.

I am called Walter Mosley, and this is my cold, hard, unbelievable truth...

PART ONE

THE CURSE OF CADILLAC SLIM

CHAPTER ONE

The shit hit the fan in the fall of '92...

Before that, I was merely existing—a kid with no roots, no purpose, and no path drifting through the foster care system like a leaf on the wind. I never really thought about who I was or where I came from. Why would I? As far as I knew, I was just another throwaway kid, bouncing from one foster home to another. But all that changed with one conversation in Sergeant Thelonious Wilson's office.

I was 12 years old then—a scrawny little bastard who didn't belong anywhere and had seen a bit too much. For weeks, I'd been on the run, hiding in the potholed streets of Chicago after escaping my fourth foster home in seven years, the Russell family.

The South Side was my playground and prison. By day, I navigated the crowded sidewalks, my jeans worn through at the knees, my sandy afro a tangled mess, and my mismatched shoes scuffing against the cracked pavement. Being a kid in that condition should've marked me as a target, but most people's eyes slid past me as if I were invisible. At night, I found refuge inside an old abandoned school bus parked in Bronzeville, somewhere on Cottage Grove. Its rusty frame groaned with each gust of wind, the musty smell of decay filling my nostrils, but it was a shelter from storms and a hideout from street gangs and prying adults who might've dragged my ass back into the system.

My street smarts kept me alive. Each morning, I'd splash water on my face from public fountains, the icy shock a brutal wake-up call. I'd sneak into fast-food joints, using rough paper towels and watered-down soap to scrub away the sticky grime of the streets. At Aldi, I'd hover near the carts, offering to return them for customers. The jingle of quarters in my pocket was a minor victory, each coin a potential meal of Cocoa Bars or Hot Cheese Doodles. Other days, I'd resort to dumpster diving, the rancid smell making my eyes water as I searched for half-eaten burgers or bruised apples like they were buried treasure.

It was a hard life, but it was mine. Being homeless beat being farmed like cattle through the foster care system, fighting traumatized kids every day, and being told what to do by unqualified adults whose only job duty was pretending to care. I'd much rather live on my own, even if that meant sleeping on that funky old bus, washing my ass with bathroom hand soap, wearing the same holey, funky clothes every day, pissing in alleys, and eating trash. I scraped by, but I was free.

Weeks passed before they caught me. They hauled my bony ass to an Englewood Police station, the cuffs biting into my wrists as they chained me to a bench. The seat was a canvas of urban life—gang tags, chewing gum, drawings of dicks etched into the wood. For hours, I watched them bring in other kids—mostly high schoolers with nowhere to go, their skin a roadmap of tattoos, their eyes hard and mean-mugging everyone who passed. We all waited our turn to see the old, fat police officer tasked with handling the neighborhood's chronic truancy problem.

This wasn't my first rodeo with Sergeant Thelonious Wilson. He always seemed to take a personal interest in my case. A strange bond had formed between us, despite him working for my arch-nemesis, the system. I never learned to show it, but over time, I grew to respect the old man. He'd offer nuggets of wisdom, share his lunch when my stomach growled too loud, and recommended books that opened my eyes to new worlds. Best of all, he listened. Whether or not I had something important to say, the old, fat police officer was patient and kind, unlike most other adults I'd known.

When I walked into his office, Wilson had already settled into his creaky chair, the leather protesting under his weight. The room was a cramped cave of knowledge, shelves groaning under the weight of thick, musty-smelling books. The walls behind his chair were a patchwork of awards, ribbons, and medals—a shiny wallpaper of pride. A withered pothos plant hung from the ceiling, its dried leaves a silent witness to countless stories told in this room.

The office fan whirred weakly, doing little to dispel the stuffy air. Wilson mopped his brow with a handkerchief, his breathing labored from the heat and his weight. Despite his imposing size, there was a gentleness in his eyes as he looked at me.

"You again?" he wheezed, his face scrunching into an ugly frown as he flipped through my truancy file. "Another Marshall boy... bites the dust."

I leaned closer, trying to sneak a peek at the file, but it was just out of reach. "Marshall boy?"

Wilson squinted at the pages, his finger tracing each line. "I'd always hoped for better from you, kid." He shook his head, disappointment etched in the lines of his face.

I half-stood, reaching for the folder. "You must be looking at the wrong case files."

Wilson's hand came down like a gavel, swatting mine away. His look alone was enough to make me sink back into my seat.

"Don't argue with me, kid. You're a Marshall boy," he insisted, his voice gravelly. "An obvious descendant of that snake, Cadillac Slim. I was there when you were born, working the night shift at St. Bernard Hospital."

I snickered, more out of confusion than amusement. "Who?"

Wilson's nose wrinkled, like he smelled something foul. "Your grandfather, that's who. A no-good, slick-talking, evil, manipulating son of a bitch from back in the day. He's been dead for 13 years and we've still got a task force cleaning his mess."

I forced out a laugh, slapping my knee for effect. "What kind of name is Cadillac Slim? That don't even sound like a real person."

Wilson's face remained impassive, waiting for my fake laughter to die down. When silence fell, he looked me dead in the eye. "You have his eyes, his nose, and his attitude problems. You hide your hands in your pockets like him, too. And that look on your face, like you know everything? That's a perfect match for Slim's old signature sly."

Wilson shifted in his chair, the leather creaking under his weight. He took a moment to catch his breath before continuing, "Look here, kiddo," he said, tapping the file with a thick finger. "According to this, Walter Mosley ain't your real name. A CPS worker named M. Bird signed this file. Looks like she named you after her favorite author until your family came forward to claim you." He let out a wheezy chuckle. "She don't know what I know."

And that's when it happened for the very first time. An icy wave of sadness crashed over me, sudden and merciless. The world descended to a grayness, leaving me feeling hollow and heavy all at once. Wilson's words punched through my chest, stealing the air from my lungs. My mind fogged over, palms slick with sweat. The fluorescent lights flickered. Or maybe that was just in my head.

No name? It took a piece of me.

Wilson's eyes glistened as he read on, tears threatening to spill despite his best efforts. Whatever was in that file was enough to crack even this hardened cop's facade. A lump formed in my throat. I felt sorry that he had to feel sorry for me.

"Okay! THAT'S IT!" Wilson cleared his throat. He slammed a hand on his desk and contorted his face into a goofy expression, clearly trying to lighten the mood. It worked—I laughed at the old pig despite everything.

Before I could respond, Wilson reached into his desk drawer and pulled out a wrapped sandwich. "Here," he said gruffly, sliding it across the desk. "You look like you haven't eaten in days."

I took the sandwich, feeling a mix of gratitude and stubbornness. Despite myself, I felt a warmth spreading in my chest at Wilson's gesture. It was more than most adults had ever done for me.

He slammed the file shut and leaned forward, fingers laced together on the desktop. Just as he opened his mouth to speak, the phone rang, making us both jump.

"What's up? Yeah... Okay... Okay... He'll be right out."

Wilson hung up and turned back to me. "Your foster mom's here to pick you up, but first, I want to tell you a story."

I slumped in my chair, arms folded, bottom lip jutting out. "Shit, man... I'm ready to bounce."

The cop met my tantrum with that blank stare of his, patient and unyielding. It was a look that could make a kid feel small for acting out. I straightened up. "What kind of story?"

"It's the most heartbreaking story I know," Wilson said, his voice heavy with emotion he was clearly trying to hide. He leaned forward, his chair groaning in protest. "And

13

unfortunately, kid, it's a story about you."

CHAPTER TWO

Word on the streets was that my grandfather, Cadillac Slim, had fathered dozens of children, but only claimed two as his sons: Sage, the oldest, whom Slim trusted and bragged about most, and Melvin, the baby boy still trying to earn his gangster father's approval. Both boys were born only 8 months apart, their mothers strangers to each other.

The brothers learned the family business together at a crazy young age—grifting men and women, counterfeiting money, and running schemes that could've gotten them killed before their bodies had grown big enough to drive. Slim was their leader, a tall, lanky, weasel motherfucker with a demeanor as cold as an icicle. He was treated like some kind of neighborhood anti-hero, infamous for the strange influence he held over people, using them as pawns in his grand schemes to do and have whatever he desired.

The Marshall Boys, as they came to be known, thrived for years, navigating through Chicago's shadows. They cruised through neighborhoods, bringing mad drama and chaos wherever they went, yet somehow earning praise from the very people they exploited. Slim, Sage, and Melvin had money stashed in so many places that they often forgot where; sharing not a dime with anyone but themselves.

In the spring of 1978, The Marshall Boys' world tilted on its axis when Sage fell in love with a target: Laura Mosley, daughter of an A.M.E. Church pastor. Laura was a beacon of light in Sage's shadow world—a kind, bold, and adventurous college girl, with skin the color of rich milk chocolate and a perfectly shaped brown afro. There was a fire in her, a spark of mischief, and a depth of kindness that drew people in. I was told that her laugh could illuminate the Roosevelt Street subway station.

Sage was immediately smitten. In Laura's presence, the allure of his old life—the lying, cheating, and stealing alongside his father and brother—suddenly lost its appeal. He yearned for something more, something pure. He wanted to do right by Laura, to shower her with genuine love and affection, to protect her, and to become the great man she deserved.

So Sage made the hardest decision of his life: he walked away. Said "fuck it" to the only life he'd ever known and dedicated himself to forging a clean, honest path. I can only imagine how difficult it must have been for him to turn his back on his father and brother, the only family he'd ever had. But Laura spoke life into Sage; she wasn't shrouded in the death and dishonesty that had defined his existence. With her, the crushing guilt Sage had carried for years was left behind with the hell he'd finally found the courage to leave.

Melvin, left alone with Cadillac Slim, felt the weight of his brother's absence the most. The warmth and protection

Sage had always provided were gone, replaced by Slim's cold expectations and harsh criticisms. Melvin threw himself into the family business, desperate to fill the void Sage had left. But no matter how hard he tried, he always felt like he was falling short.

After living the dream for a few years, Sage and Laura began to experience the usual lows that often come when trying to sync as a couple. On top of the uncomfortable task of compromise, agreeing to disagree, and trying to respect each other's boundaries, financial difficulties arose as well. Bills piled up, and moods went south. It was during this time, in early 1980, that Laura discovered she was pregnant.

In an effort to alleviate the financial stress, Sage took on a second job tossing boxes at a local bread factory. He worked long hours and was exhausted by the time he came home. The increased workload left Sage unable to spend as much quality time with his wife as he desired, leaving him frustrated and longing for her companionship, while Laura felt lonely and neglected when she needed him most.

Laura's transformation was gradual, but unmistakable. The warmth in her eyes dimmed, replaced by a hardness that Sage had never seen before. Her infectious laugh became rare, and her words took on a sharp edge. The scent of her favorite jasmine perfume, once a comforting presence in their home, was replaced by the acrid smell of cigarette smoke and bottom shelf liquor.

This emotional distance fueled their arguments and bickering, which had become a frequent part of their relationship. The carefree, loving, once-in-a-lifetime vibe they once shared had been buried under fear, guilt, and resentment for decisions they'd made.

In the late months of her difficult pregnancy, late September, the couple had their biggest fight to date. Laura had been coming home late more often, with the same drunken smile on her face and a faint scent of tobacco and musk clinging to her clothes. The Laura he had grown to love was gone. Nothing remained but a cold, distant look in her eyes. An emptiness. A long, hard glare of goodbye.

The suitcase was already packed—tucked away and hidden in her side of their closet. Laura entered the bedroom that night and came out a minute later, dragging, heaving, and lugging that suitcase with every bit of muscle she had.

Sage dropped to his knees, gazed at his woman, and begged with his arms reaching out for the suitcase. "Please don't leave me," he pleaded desperately. The rough carpet bit into his knees, and the scent of Laura's perfume mixed with something unfamiliar—a musky cologne that didn't belong to him.

Laura snatched away from her man, completely out of reach. That's when he saw it—the blood that stained his hands. He stood unsteadily, taking in the horror before him. The blood on his knees, on the floor where he'd begged for his girl, it was everywhere. A trail of crimson spots led from his knees to Laura's feet, up towards the inside of her legs.

Sage's heart pounded in his ears, his vision narrowing to a tunnel focused solely on Laura. The metallic scent of blood filled his nostrils, making his stomach churn. His hands trembled, and a cold sweat broke out across his forehead.

Laura's eyes rolled back in her head as she fell to the floor with a thud, landing on her 8-month-pregnant stomach and rolling to her side. Sage scooped her off the floor in a panic and rushed her to the hospital as fast as he could, dodging potholes running east on 47th Street, running red lights down Cottage Grove and Drexel, completely unaware of the all-black Cadillac Deville that followed closely behind.

Hospital minutes seemed to tick by like hours, every second its own special layer of wait. Sage couldn't shake off the feels. Why did Laura flip? Had he neglected his responsibilities as a man? Had he not been there for her? Was he good enough?

Sage's pacing quickened. Each step became more frenzied with every passing moment. He rubbed his hands together, tried to calm their shaking while he waited for news about his wife and unborn child. He prayed to God, vowing to become a better husband, father, and man, in return for their lives.

After Sage had grown tired of pacing and praying, he found a bench near the sliding doors of the lobby and collapsed onto it. He sat there with his elbows rested on his knees and his hands holding onto his head. Tears formed puddles on the floor by his steel-toe work boots.

Not a minute after nightfall, a man wearing flashy dark shades stepped inside the sliding doors of St. Bernard. He wore all black from head to toe, except for the eight gold rings on his fingers and a lion's head medallion that hung from a golden Cuban Link. His silk shirt was intentionally opened to show off his chest hair, dressed as if prepared for a drug deal in the back of a Miami nightclub. It was tough to recognize him at first, but as the man got closer, Sage realized it was Melvin.

His younger brother seemed to have changed for the

worse. Cadillac Slim had taught the men to always keep up appearances, to always look sharp and polished. Melvin's clothes looked expensive but worn sloppy. His hair wasn't lined, his shoes weren't crisp, his charisma was off. It seemed he'd grown shorter and rounder since the day Sage had left him for the good life of love. The once vibrant spark in Melvin's eyes had been replaced by a hardened glint, a testament to the years spent under Slim's unforgiving tutelage.

Still, it was Melvin, a flash from the past as pure as day. Without a second thought, Sage wrapped his brawny arms around Melvin, lifting him slightly off the ground.

"I'm so glad you're here, brother," Sage choked at his words, ashamed of his deeply uncontrollable tears. "I've missed you, man."

Melvin moved his head away, turned his nose up at Sage. Then he put a hand on his chest and pushed him hard enough to move him aside. "I didn't come here for you," Melvin said as the doctor simultaneously approached.

The doctor poured himself into the waiting area, covered in what seemed to have been all of Laura's blood. His eyes looked tired and defeated. He could hardly raise a breath when he broke the sad news. "I've never seen anything like it," his voice was heavy with shivers, his face aimed down at the hospital floor. "I'm sorry, Mr. Marshall. We did everything we could."

"Everything you could about what?!" Sage looked around for answers. An answer from the doctor who'd broken the sad news, an answer from the nurse who stood behind him. Sage looked around the room for an answer from the security officer who stood near the door, an answer from a woman who sat with her child, an answer from his lost little brother who'd just shown up and rejected his love. "What the fuck is going on?"

The doctor braced himself, filled his chest with air, and released it as slowly as he could. "We were able to save the baby, but, unfortunately, your wife, Laura Marshall, has passed."

The answer hit Sage like a freight train. It dropped him down to his knees once again. Tears ran wildly down the sides of his face. "Laura! My Laura," he cried out.

The answer hit Melvin like a truck. It dropped him down to his knees on the hospital floor. Tears ran wildly down the sides of his face. "Laura! My Laura," he cried out.

Sage turned to his brother. He watched the snot run down from Melvin's nose to his mouth, blending with tears and thick saliva that hung like a string. The math was finally adding up: the late-night whispers on the phone, unusual mood swings, mean attitude, and coming home reeking of tequila and weed.

"You slept with Laura?" Sage grunted and cringed as if he'd lost a million dollars in a street fight. "You've been fucking my wife?"

Sage, in shock, watched his hands tremble in front of his

eyes. He closed his eyes, took a breath, and started counting aloud, "1, 2, 3, 4..." searching for a way to stay calm. His jaw clenched, muscles twitching beneath his skin. The fluorescent lights seemed to grow brighter and harsher, as a roaring built in his ears.

Melvin must have felt the ground rumble, like the vibrations of a volcano close to erupting. He removed himself from the danger of Sage's long arm-reach. He dipped off slowly and cautiously, straight toward the delivery room where the baby was left alone, crying in an incubator, still covered in his mother's blood and cheesy afterbirth while the doctors and nurses all bathed themselves in the shock of Laura's death.

"You left," Melvin said. "You were my brother. You were all I ever had, and you left." He cried as he picked up the baby.

"25, 26, 27..." Sage was still counting aloud as Melvin returned to the hall holding Laura's bloody baby in his arms.

"You left me alone with that evil motherfucker," Melvin

spat, his eyes burning with years of pent-up rage and resentment. "I had to watch him die old, demented, and angry. His mind wasn't right, couldn't remember me half the time."

Melvin's voice cracked slightly, betraying the pain beneath his anger. "Do you know what it's like to have your own father look at you like a stranger? To have the man who taught you everything, who you spent your whole life trying to please, suddenly not even recognize your face?"

He paused, his fists clenching and unclenching at his sides. "And you, Sage? You were the one he remembered. Even when he couldn't recall his own name, he'd call out for you. His last dying wish was for you to come back to us."

Melvin's words hung in the air, heavy with the weight of abandonment and unfulfilled expectations. "You took everything from me when you left, and now I'm taking everything from you."

Sage barely registered Melvin's words or his sadness. His mind was still reeling from Laura's death, the betrayal still slicing his heart. He stared, numb and disbelieving, as Melvin cradled the newborn in his arms.

Melvin held the baby close to his heart, rocking it gently. "Shh, shh, it's okay," he cooed, his voice suddenly soft and soothing. "Daddy's got you." He planted a gentle kiss on the baby's forehead, all the while keeping his eyes locked on Sage, a taunting, evil stare that dared his brother to respond with emotion.

"Goo-goo, ga-ga," Melvin babbled. "Daddy's here now, isn't he? Yes, he is."

Sage had stopped counting at 50, his attempt at calming himself long forgotten. He turned his focus to his tightly clenched fists, knuckles holding nothing but contained rage and grief. Then he looked up again, forced to confront the reality before him: Melvin holding Laura's newborn son, the child that should have been undoubtedly his.

The baby, small and fragile, wrapped in a bloodstained blanket, its tiny face scrunched up in a cry that seemed to echo through the hallway. The sound pierced through Sage's shock, woke his ass up to the sight of his woman lying dead on a birthing bed, and his child all wrapped up in the hands of a nightmare.

"Take your hands off my son," Sage growled, his voice in a low and dangerous rumble.

Melvin's eyes glinted with malice. "This is my son, fool! You pro'bly haven't hit that in months."

Those words were the match that lit the keg of Sage's rage. All the pain he had felt combined into a physical fury that consumed him entirely. His eyes turned red, the world around him fading away except for Melvin and the baby. Sage bit down on his tongue, barely containing the roar of anguish and anger that threatened to tear from his throat.

Before Melvin could move to drop the baby, Sage lunged at his brother. His hands, cold and bare, found Melvin's throat. With a strength born of grief and betrayal, Sage forced Melvin back into the wall and then down to the floor. His grip tightened, fingers digging into the soft flesh of his brother's neck, even as Melvin clutched the child like a football.

Sage continued to squeeze his brother's throat until his legs stopped kicking, then squeezed a little longer and harder, just to make sure the job was done. It took four doctors and two police officers to pry Sage away from his brother's lifeless body. One of those officers was a younger, more fit Sergeant Wilson before the years of stress and glazed donuts had taken their toll.

Four, maybe five more cops came to help contain Sage's rage. He was arrested and charged with murder, his world crumbling around him. The police, perhaps sensing the depth of his anguish or fearing his strength, thrashed him before taking him away, although he offered no resistance. The legal proceedings that followed were a blur of grief and confusion for Sage, who could barely comprehend the charges against him. In the end, due to the circumstances of the crime and his fragile mental state, he was found not guilty by reason of insanity and committed to the University of Chicago Hospital for Mental Health.

If you were to delve into the records of this place and do a thorough investigation, you would find that my story connects. Sage Henry Marshall, the man who stands accused of his brother's demise, remains imprisoned in this very institution, a shadow of his former self. The man who once walked away from a life of crime for love now walks the sterile halls of this mental hospital, trapped in a prison of his own mind.

But there's more to this story. Possibly, with a DNA test, or by contacting the station where the old fat policeman, Sergeant Wilson, had worked for 30 years, we can prove that I was that baby, born on that fateful day, in the midst of chaos and tragedy. Sage Henry Marshall, patient #3235A, could very well be my biological father.

CHAPTER THREE

Growing up in foster care was a grueling, never-ending nightmare. The constant upheaval and instability left me with a lifetime of emotional scars and abandonment issues that still haunt me today. I could never find comfort. Each time I was uprooted and tossed into a home of strangers made me feel like a misfit, an outsider, a charity case, a burden.

That's why I kept to myself. I didn't speak many words until I was six years old. I'd say yes, no, maybe give a shoulder shrug to answer a question, but nothing more than a point of the finger. If I really didn't want to be bothered, I'd just stare in silence until the person asking questions left my face. The consequence was that most adults believed I was dumb. I often heard them say I was "L.D.", short for 'learning disability', and I never cared enough to defend myself. In fact, I was called stupid so much that I believed it, even though I'd taught myself to read, write poetry, count money, and had developed tactical thinking skills all before my 7th birthday.

Each placement brought new terrors and uncertainties. Every foster home had its way of making me feel like a captive. I am not the best prisoner, so I ran away from every foster home I ever lived in.

My first escape was a moment of pure liberation. I was seven years old.

Those foster parents took the straight-up approach. They often treated me differently than their regular kids. When I entered the room, they would keep secrets and whisper, and unofficially diagnose me with ADD and ADHD. I was even coerced into taking Ritalin pills they got from other kids who may have actually needed them. They looked funny. They smelled funny. All of them. Their condescending tones, their smirks, their snarls, and their eyes made me feel like a reject.

I couldn't stomach their food or the words they used to portray me, so I bounced. Couldn't do it. Had to go.

I managed twelve long hours before I was caught, and I wasn't afraid. I ran away from that family every weekend until they gave me back to the system. And I didn't stop there. Potentially adopted or not, I ran from the foster homes, from the group home, from the orphanage, from the schools. I got my ass up out of there. Each time I ran, I stayed away longer and longer, spending days, weeks, and sometimes months before that old fat police officer would catch me and drag my ass backward. He never gave up on me. I kept running away, and Sergeant Wilson kept catching me.

Wilson was a complicated figure in my life, a constant reminder of the thin line between compassion and control. He was the only person who ever bothered to come looking for me when I ran away, and for that, I was both grateful and resentful. He scolded me for my reckless behavior, but he was also the one who brought me food and clean clothes and tried to reassure me that I had a future beyond the foster care system.

At times, I listened to his words, considering the possibility that maybe, just maybe, I could make something great of myself. But more often than not, I pushed back against his attempts to help me, rejecting his pity and charity. It was a constant battle between us, a tug-of-war between the longing for human connection and the fear of being trapped by it.

Despite my doubts and reservations, there was something about Officer Wilson that I couldn't ignore. He was the only adult I could truly respect, the only one who seemed to understand what I was going through. He's the first human to look upon me with genuine concern and wish for the best. In a world where so many people had let me down, where too many people who didn't care about me had the power to dictate my life for a paycheck, Officer Wilson stood out as a beacon of hope, a flawed but well-meaning ally in my ongoing battle for freedom.

The older I got, the more I visited Officer Wilson, seeking his company and the stories he told about Slim, Sage, Melvin, and Laura. He spoke to me with a level of understanding that I had never experienced before, sharing his own experiences of loneliness and rejection. He too was a product of the foster care system who knew what it was like to be unwanted, to grow up without a family, without significance, without a home. I listened to his tales like my life depended on them, finding comfort in the fact that someone else had gone through what I was living.

Wilson taught me mostly of Slim, the brutal conqueror. Most of Slim's tales were downright disturbing, how he preyed on the vulnerable and took advantage of those who didn't learn what they needed to know about their money, or themselves. But even as he spoke of Slim's misdeeds, he did so in a way that made the man sound like a hero, someone to be admired and revered. The Genghis Khan of the po-pimps and hustlers of Chicago. I felt a sense of pride in knowing that I was connected to such a legendary figure, even if he wasn't perfect. Wilson had this bright idea that maybe I could use my family history for good. He said I had smarts within my DNA. It made me more determined than ever to use my own wits to make my way in the world.

The day I turned 18, September 21st, 1998, I was finally freed from the foster care system. It is still, to this day, one of the greatest moments in my life. I was ready to live on the streets, to stay inside that old school bus and hustle my way up if I had to, but Wilson had it all planned out. As a gift and token of my newfound freedom, I inherited a sum of Cadillac Slim's money, his condo in Hyde Park, and that cool-ass 1976 Cadillac Deville Convertible from the police impound, which had all been saved and preserved for me by Wilson himself.

The moment I laid eyes on that car, I couldn't help but shed a tear. I remember Wilson removing the cover to unveil the Caddy and tossing me the keys. He said, "It's all practically yours anyway, since you're the only known descendant of Slim we have on paper. Now, you can finally leave me the hell alone, and I can finally retire from the Chicago Police. No more chasing you down."

I thanked him, and he followed by saying, "If you really want to thank me, take some of that money and enroll yourself in school."

"I will," I lied.

With my newfound freedom and inheritance, I stood at a crossroads. The world, suddenly wide open, brimmed with possibilities I'd never dared to imagine. Yet, amidst all these opportunities, one thought refused to let go: Sage Marshall, the man I suspected was my biological father.

For days, I grappled with indecision. Part of me wanted to forget the past, to embrace my freedom and never look back. But a stronger part, one rooted deep in my soul, yearned for answers, for connection, for a sense of belonging that had eluded me my entire life. I spent sleepless nights pacing in

Slim's old condo, torn between the fear of what I might discover and the need to confront the truth.

In the end, my roots pulled me too strongly to ignore. I realized that to move forward, I needed to understand where I came from. With a mix of trepidation and excitement, I resolved to find Sage Marshall and face the truth of my origins, whatever it might be.

That first day of freedom, I cruised down Lake Shore Drive in Cadillac Slim's DeVille, the wind whipping through my hair, and I felt an exhilarating sense of liberation. The car, a black beast with gleaming paint, plush leather seats, and a purring engine, was a symbol of the control I finally had over my own destiny. For the first time in my life, I could go anywhere, do anything, and no one could stop me.

But as I drove, my thoughts kept circling back to Sage. A whirlwind of emotions swept through me. What would he look like? Would he recognize me? Would he even want to see me? The uncertainty was both terrifying and thrilling, yet I knew this was a journey I had to take.

When I pulled into the parking lot of the mental institution on October 6, 1998, I was filled with a mix of nerves and determination. The building loomed gray and foreboding, matching the overcast sky above. I hesitated in the car, my heart racing and hands trembling. The seat beneath me felt sticky with sweat, a testament to my anxiety. I rummaged through the car, searching for anything to calm my frayed nerves, but found only remnants of the past: pictures of women with wild afros, a snapshot of Slim, Melvin, and Sage, and an empty, mysterious vial of cologne.

The bottle was a dusty blue, its label faded and peeling. A few drops of its musky scent clung to the clogged nozzle. The cologne, rumored to have mystical powers, had appeared in various stories throughout my life, whispers of its ability to control thoughts and actions. Though I dismissed these superstitions as fantasy, I couldn't shake the unease as I sprayed the last dregs onto my neck and arms. The bottle felt like it held a strange power, one I couldn't quite grasp.

Shaking off the feeling, I tossed the empty bottle in the back

and watched it roll to the floor.

CHAPTER FOUR

There's a woman who works here, at The University of Chicago Hospital for Mental Health, this awful place of mental abidance. Her name is Margie Jackson, and she's likely the director of bullshit here at this facility.

You might know her. She's the one who screeches into the parking lot around noon every workday, blasting "We Gonna Make It" from her cherry-red Range Rover, the bass thumping loud enough to reach us patients out in the yard. Margie wasn't always like this. When I first came here a few years back, she was a different person—a woman in scrubs and white sneakers, working the desk and following orders. But now, she's moved up to some higher position that nobody really understands, wearing business suits, sitting in a nice corner office, and being more insufferable than ever.

I just want to say, from the bottom of my heart: fuck Margie.

Margie gives the patients here more trouble than we need. She's often dismissive, uses a patronizing tone, and never takes the time to really listen to us. She pranks us too— knocking over chessboards, hiding Captain Roger's juice box, and who knows what else. Most days, when a patient loses it, when someone is teetering on the edge, it's likely because of something she did. And it's not just the patients who can't stand her—the nurses, doctors, and even the kind lady in the cafeteria all loathe Margie.

Fire Margie Jackson.

The Margie Jackson of today isn't the same Margie I met when I first set foot in this place. Back then, she wasn't the devil. She was different—someone who almost seemed to care.

I remember that day well. I walked into the hospital, my

nerves on edge, bracing myself for my first meeting with Sage. I didn't know what to expect, but the first person I saw was Margie Jackson, a young receptionist back then. She greeted me with a smile that eased my tension, pulling me into the lobby, distracting me from my fears. It was the first smile I'd ever seen without any hidden agenda. She didn't know much about me, so her smile felt genuine, the first one I ever believed.

She was cool then—looked me in the eyes when she spoke, even touched my hand when she led me down the hall towards the visiting room. As we walked, Margie read Sage's file, warning me that he had been diagnosed with a form of schizophrenia, that he suffered from paranoid delusions and self-harmed whenever it rained. She told me these awful things, but nothing sounded too bad when it was spoken by her. Little nice Margie, the girl who grew up to show off the blue and pink tattoo on her right breast, was once the thoughtful, delicate, college girl who walked me down these long halls and introduced me to two large and intimidating men and asked them to protect me on my visit with Sage.

Young, thoughtful, Margie was very specific in her instructions: never stare directly into Sage's eyes, never turn your back on him, and don't get too close. She also told me that Sage hadn't spoken a word in 18 years. But I clung to hope—maybe the picture I'd found in the Caddy or the possibility that Sage could be my father would get him to talk.

Margie and the guards led me into a small room with a large, round table and two chairs. The room smelled of lavender, and the carpet matched the scent with its soft, soothing color. The walls were covered in drawings— children's art, vibrant and colorful, made with crayons, markers, even fingernails. It gave the room a strange warmth. The lighting was dim, with just a few lamps casting a soft glow, making the room feel more inviting than it probably was. There was a small window, but it was covered by a thick curtain, blocking out the outside world. "Wait here, Sweetie,"

Margie said before she and the guards left, closing the door behind them.

I took a deep breath and a moment to center my nerves. The room was small and plain, but the artwork on the walls and the scent of lavender made it feel like a sanctuary. I sat down in one of the chairs and waited for Margie and the guards to bring Sage into the room.

Twenty minutes passed, and then I heard three loud knocks before the door creaked open, the sound bouncing around the small room. The two large guards entered first, telling me to move to the far side of the room until Sage was seated and calm. They looked serious, sweat darkening the pits of their shirts. I nodded, my heart pounding, and moved as they instructed.

Sage's eyes locked onto mine the moment he entered, as if he recognized me, though it was our first time meeting. I had expected something out of 'Silence of the Lambs,' but Sage seemed almost normal, aside from needing a shave and a hot comb. His expression was unreadable, but there was no aggression in his demeanor. He sat down at the table without any trouble, interlocking his fingers and waiting. The guards made sure it was safe for me to join him. So I did. Sat all the way on the other side of the big round table.

I couldn't find the words. None.

Sweat began to bead and roll down my face. Completely aware that I was violating Marge's first warning of not making eye contact with Sage, but I couldn't look away. He didn't seem to mind; instead, he squinted an eye, still not saying a word.

Finally, I took a deep breath and spoke. "Hi, people call me Walter Mosley. I'm 18 years old. I am the son of Laura Marshall, and I wanted to meet you today because I think you're my father." The words came out slurred like I was just learning to speak.

Sage stared at me, unmoving, his face still blank. I felt a knot tightening in my stomach, but I had to keep going.

"I know this might be hard to believe, but I found a picture of you." I reached into my pocket. "I've been looking for answers about my father for a long time, and I think you might be him." I paused, my voice trembling. "Hope it's you."

I pulled out the old photo and slid it across the table to Sage. He lifted his hands, the cuffs clinking as he grabbed it. Sage looked down at the picture, his eyes staying on it until a tear dropped onto the print. I waited for him to say something, but he remained silent, his gaze fixed hard on the photo.

"I plan to visit you sometime, Pops. Just to spend time together. Maybe one day you'll talk to me. Maybe I could learn something from you. Maybe we can work towards getting you out of here," I said, my voice almost a whisper.

That's when Sage finally looked up at me. His eyes seemed to come alive, like a child's after hearing a promise. He reached out, his hands extending toward mine. I glanced at the guards, unsure if this was allowed. "Is this okay?" I asked. They shrugged, but their body language shifted, growing tense, their hands hovering near their waists, ready to step in. A knock on the window signaled that it was fine for me to go ahead, but the guards stayed on high alert.

Sage's hands told a story of their own—hard, beaten, and calloused. They were the hands of a man who'd only known push-ups, knuckles that had punched through walls, nails that were chewed down to nubs. I could feel a lifetime of pain in his grip. I held on as long as I could before I had to pull away.

And then Sage broke down. He cried—really cried. The kind of sobbing that releases years of sorrow and grief. He stood up from the table, opened his arms, and thanked me with his tear-filled eyes.

In complete disregard for Margie's warning, I leaped across the table and embraced the gestured hug received from Sage. The guards reacted immediately, taking a step forward, their hands reaching out to separate us. But they hesitated, seeing the seemingly peaceful nature of our embrace. I could feel him relax in my arms as if he had been longing for this simple human connection since they put him away. I held him close, and felt a sense of warmth and comfort wash inside me, but as he took a deep inhale, something shifted. The scent of that musky cologne had triggered something in Sage, taking him back to a memory, a traumatic one. It wasn't long before Sage's embrace had turned into a suffocating bear hug.

With my nose buried deep in his chest, I felt the suffocating pressure of my father's embrace, like a vice pressing tightly around me. His towering presence loomed over my 5'11" 175-pound frame. I struggled desperately, both arms flailed to break free. My breath was getting shallow by the second, lungs crying out to expand.

With each passing moment, my breaths became shallower, my lungs crying out for air as his grip tightened. The world around me blurred, and panic clawed at the edges of my consciousness. I tried to call out for help, but the words were caught in my constricted throat. My heart pounded, matching the rhythm of my futile attempts to escape.

The guards sprang into action, their earlier hesitation forgotten. They wedged themselves between us, prying us apart with calculated force. My father's eyes were filled with a mix of desperation and rage.

More people poured into the room: nurses, doctors, and security guards. Then Margie ran inside with a juicy syringe, jumped on Sage's back, and stuck him in the back of his neck. They finally managed to separate us.

I stumbled backward, gasping for breath and clutching my chest, watched and listened to Sage speak his first words in 18 years.

"Let me go," he screamed and fought for my life as he struggled to break from the guards. "Kill that motherfucker," he wailed. "He's gonna curse us all."

Sage's voice was raw and hoarse from disuse. He reached out, grabbing at me with wild eyes as I shrank into the corner of the small room. Nothing but a large round table and two tiring guards kept Sage from pulling off my neck with his hands. I prayed the shot would kick in soon.

"You're not my son! You're not my son!"

Before I knew it, Sage was unconscious, his body going limp in the arms of the guards who let him fall to the floor. They caught their breaths and carried him out of the room, his head hanging down, his arms swinging lifelessly at his sides. I watched him go, unable to move or speak.

I stumbled backward, fell into the chair, and jumped up to my feet in a panic. But nice Margie returned in the doorway and waved me to safety. "This kind of thing happens all the time," she lied. But I couldn't shake the feeling of disappointment.

Sage was not the father I had hoped for.

CHAPTER FIVE

The rain came down in torrents, each drop soaking through my clothes and hair, merging with the river of tears on my face. Cold water seeped through to my skin, numbing the tips of my nose, ears, and fingers, but the chill of the storm couldn't compete with the loneliness that gripped me after meeting with Sage.

I had parked all the way in the last row of the vast parking lot, far from the hospital's entrance, surrounded by a sea of empty spaces. The distant streetlights flickered weakly through the downpour, their light reflecting off the puddles that had formed in the cracked asphalt.

I unlocked the Caddy, sat inside, and slammed the door behind me, shutting out the storm but not the turmoil inside me. The car's interior felt like a sanctuary, but also a cage, trapping me with my thoughts. I pulled out my Nokia flip phone, its screen faintly glowing in the dim light, and dialed the only person I knew. When Wilson didn't answer, I felt a small sense of relief. I sat there, in the parking lot, for a few more minutes, listening to the relentless downpour of rain and distant thunder, staring through the windshield at the blurred outlines of the hospital, the raindrops racing each other down the glass, hoping it would help calm my nerves…

The shit didn't work.

I could still hear Sage's gritty voice inside of my head. "You're not my son." The words echoed. Each repetition is a fresh, deep wound. My mind raced, replaying the scene over and over. What had I expected? A warm embrace? A tearful reunion? Instead, I got rejection and violence.

I'd spent my whole life running from connections, and the one time I reached out, I got burned. It wasn't long before the panic set in. A deep, dark shadow seemed to close in around me, thicker than the storm clouds that unleashed rain all over my car. My skin flushed hot and cold at once, tunnel vision narrowing my world to the confines of the driver's seat. My heart pounded so hard it felt like it might burst through my chest. A bitter taste filled my mouth—stomach acid and undigested food clawing its way up, burning my throat and nostrils. Muscle spasms seized my ribs, each breath coming in short, painful gasps. The air felt thick with hair-like thorns, prickling every inch of my skin.

Completely lost it, I slammed my hands against the steering wheel, again and again, shouting curses into the parking lot at everyone I saw, my voice barely audible over the pounding rain, but the horn of the car was loud and clear. I bit down hard on my bottom lip until I tasted the blood.

Passersby, their faces blurred by the downpour, glanced into the car as they hurried by, but no one gave a damn enough to stop. They had the rain to excuse them.

While inside my fit of anger, the glove box popped open,

and a bottle of cologne fell out onto the floor. I picked up the bottle, confused. It looked like the same cologne I had used before, but it was in pristine condition. The blue glass seemed more vibrant, almost glowing in the dim light.

Curious, I climbed into the back seat, searching frantically for the empty bottle I was sure I had tossed back there earlier. But it was nowhere to be found. I searched every crevice, every nook, but came up empty-handed. Had I just imagined tossing it back there? Is my mind playing tricks on me? I sat there, scratching the top of my head in shock.

"What in the hell are you doing back there?" A laughing voice questioned, along with a few hard knocks on the window. It was Margie, standing in the rain with her hands shielding her eyes, trying her best to see through the extra foggy windows of my car.

At that point, I had gone far beyond a panic attack. Couldn't speak. Couldn't see. Brain had gone foggy as well.

Margie stood outside my window getting wetter and

wetter, hair uncovered, shoes being soaked. "Go home, Mr. Mosley. You're scaring everyone," she warned me, loud enough to compete with the hard pouring rain and the car door between us.

I dropped the bottle of cologne on the floor, used my foot to push it under the front seat. Used the same foot and kicked open the back door before I slid to the far side of the long back seat. I was not in the mood for smiling, but I tried anyway, forgetting there was blood in my teeth. "Get in," I insisted, my voice creaking and cracking. "You're getting wet."

Her laughter quickly flipped to a scream. Her eyes bulged when she stumbled, fell back, and sat in a puddle. Said, "Hell no! You...Creep!" then jumped up and ran away at breakneck speed.

I didn't linger to find out if she called the cops. Flipped over to the front seat, fired up the Caddy, and let the engine roar hard as I zoomed out of the parking lot, pushing at the limits of the Caddy's top speed. I didn't slow down until I made my way to Lake Shore Drive, then cruised in disgust of myself, all the way back to the Hyde Park condo.

The drive seemed endless. Each streetlight I passed illuminated my reflection in the rearview mirror—a stranger stared back at me. Who was I now? The hopeful kid looking for his father was gone, replaced by... what? A reject? A disappointment? Sage's words kept echoing in my head, mixing with all the other rejections I'd faced in my life. Foster parents who'd given up on me, teachers who'd written me off, and now my own father.

When I approached the Hyde Park neighborhood, the rain let up a bit. The elegant brownstones and tree-lined streets seemed to mock my internal turmoil. Students from the University of Chicago hurried along the sidewalks, their lives full of purpose and direction. I felt like an imposter in this world of academia and culture. What right did I have to be here, in this fancy neighborhood, driving this fancy car? I was just a foster kid playing dress-up in someone else's life.

The condo wasn't bad. It had a vintage grand lobby with lots of large mirrors, gold crown molding, and winter-green carpet. The elevator jerked when it lifted and slammed when it came to a stop. The unit was 1200 square feet, with two bedrooms, a large living space, a dining room, and a small kitchen fair enough to make a good meal. I could see the best parts of the beach, the Jackson Park basketball courts, the Museum of Science and Industry, and more from my living room window. I could tell the place had been nice way back in the day, but it was hard for a kid like me to appreciate it. The car, the crib, the money, and that musky-smelling manly cologne I'd inherited just didn't feel real.

I stood at the window, watching the last remnants of daylight fade. The lights of the neighborhood twinkled, and I could see people gathering at a nearby bar. Their laughter drifted up, a reminder of the connections I lacked. I ordered a pizza, more out of habit than hunger, and settled in for a long night of self-loathing.

As darkness fell, I found myself drawn to the bathroom mirror. The face that looked back at me was haggard, eyes red-rimmed from crying. I barely recognized myself. Who was I trying to be? What was I even doing here? I thought about Sage, locked away in that institution. Was that my future? Was I doomed to end up just like him, alone and trapped in my own mind?

I opened the cabinet to find toothpaste and froze. There, on the first shelf, directly in the center, sat that damned bottle of cologne. The same one I'd pushed beneath the seat of my car and left there to die. My hand trembled as I reached for it, half-expecting it to vanish like a mirage.

But it was solid, real. I felt it calling for me.

I remembered the story of how my mother had been seduced by it, and how it had ruined Sage's life. I thought about how much it scared me to find the strange bottle restored in my glove box. Thought about how much rage Sage had felt when he smelled it on me. But then, I thought about how nice Margie acted when I first arrived to visit with Sage, and how repulsed she was the moment the scent had worn off. The memory of her disgust, her fear, had suddenly stung me again. "Creep," she'd called me. Was that all I was?

Almost without conscious thought, I removed the bottle cap and sprayed it on myself. The scent enveloped me, an intoxicating mix of musk and something wilder, more primal. It was an animal's musk, not synthetic. Like a deer was sacrificed just to brew the concoction.

The cologne seemed to seep into my pores, filling me with a confidence I'd never known. Suddenly, the idea of going out, of being around people, didn't seem so daunting. I threw on some clothes—khaki pants, Ralph Lauren polo, Air Force Ones, and a Kangol hat. Thought I was fresh. Shaved my little mustache and rubbed on extra deodorant to make sure my armpits weren't offensive.

As I headed out, I caught my reflection in the lobby mirror. For a moment, I saw a flash of someone else—was it

Slim? Sage? The image was gone in an instant, but it left me unsettled. Was I following in their footsteps? Did I even have a choice? The thought of becoming like Sage terrified me, but wasn't I already on that path? Alone, angry, lashing out at the world. But the thought of becoming like Slim... that was almost worse. Using people, manipulating them. But wasn't that what the world had done to me my whole life?

The night air was crisp, carrying the lingering scent of rain. The bar I'd seen from my window was bustling, patrons spilling out onto the sidewalk. I approached, my heart racing. A group of people stood near the entrance, laughing over some shared joke. I walked past them, close enough for them to catch my scent.

At first, nothing happened. I stood there, feeling foolish, my insecurities creeping back. But then someone turned, their eyes locking onto mine. It all felt so easy, almost effortless. Before I knew it, we were in my Cadillac, cruising through Hyde Park and winding our way downtown. The city and lakefront stretched out before us as we drove for hours, lost in the rhythm of the streets and the warmth of each other's company.

As time passed, I felt a hollow victory. This wasn't a real connection, not really. It was just another form of running, of hiding from my real problems. But what else did I have? Sage's rejection still stung, a constant reminder of my rootlessness. At least this way, for a few hours, I could pretend I was wanted, desired, and important.

Days turned into weeks, weeks into months. My routine became a cycle of cologne, superficial interactions, and fleeting connections. I met people at clubs, grocery stores, libraries—anywhere and everywhere. With each encounter, I felt a piece of myself slip away. The money piled up, but so did the weight of my actions. I'd look in the mirror and see a stranger, a man becoming more like Slim with each passing day. Was this what Sage had tried to kill me about? Is this the great curse he spoke of?

Yet I couldn't stop. These interactions were my sole source of personal triumph, the only taste of victory I knew. I'd been insulted, criticized, and controlled for so long. I'd heard so many explanations of things I wasn't good at; it was good to be admired for once. Being praised for my charm, my coolness, and the way I spoke and carried myself was my only validation in an otherwise aimless existence.

CHAPTER SIX

On the night of my 21st birthday, I found myself lying awake in bed, staring at the walls. A fine chocolate woman I'd met downtown Chicago while shopping for suits slept peacefully beside me. As I admired how the moonlight bounced off her skin, I couldn't help but reflect on the past year of my life. Twenty-one. Damn! A few years ago, I was just a lost boy searching for a father. Now, I was... what? A man? A hustler? Something in between?

The soft sound of her breathing mingled with the hum of the city outside my window. I should have felt content, maybe even happy. Here I was, living in a condo, with a beautiful woman in my bed, and money I did little to earn—yet I still felt empty inside.

I thought about Sage, about the rejection that had sent me spiraling down this path. I thought about all the women I'd been with since then, each encounter filling my pockets but leaving my soul a little more hollow.

A pizza box, champagne bottle, and cute lady panties sat near the foot of my bed, with her bra hanging from the ceiling fan, turning slowly, scenting the breeze with peony and blush. These remnants of our earlier celebration seemed almost mocking now, reminders of a lifestyle that felt increasingly hollow with each passing day.

I should have been sleeping, but I was up early, doing my usual routine of ruminating. Looking back on that moment, I'm thankful for that night of overthinking. Otherwise, I'd have missed the cries I heard—and my first chance at being saved by the girl of my dreams.

The cries were low at first, almost imperceptible. I questioned if the alcohol had fooled me or if maybe I was dreaming. But as they grew louder and more desperate, I realized they were real. Impossible to ignore.

I got up, leaving the pretty woman in the bed by herself, and walked around the bedroom with my ear to the walls, following the sound into the hallway, holding up my oversized basketball shorts with one hand. No socks, no underwear, and no t-shirt—just a skinny boy with a small bird chest and big abs, on his way to save the day.

My heart pounded in the quiet hallway. The cold floor beneath my bare feet sent shivers up my spine, or maybe that was the adrenaline kicking in. As I approached 7A, the screams grew louder, more desperate. My palms were sweaty, making it hard to keep a grip on my shorts. The air felt thick, charged with a tension I couldn't quite explain. Each step brought me closer to those haunting cries, and with each step, I felt a strange mix of fear and determination growing inside me.

I hesitated for a moment before the door. What was I doing? I barely knew my neighbors and had hardly seen them since they moved in a year ago. But something in those screams compelled me forward. No decent human being could hear cries like that and do nothing.

I banged on the door, almost dropping my shorts. "Yo, what the Fuck!?" I shouted, trying to sound tough and intimidating. I thought of Wilson when I did it.

No one answered, but I could hear someone moving behind the door.

"Open up the door, or I'm breaking it down!" I threatened; though I wasn't sure how I'd follow through.

After what felt like an eternity, the door creaked open. An older woman appeared, possibly in her mid-to-late 50s, with gray hair scattered all over her head, neatly held together by a mixture of foam and rag rollers. Her eyes were half-closed, like she'd been sitting in the darkness for days.

"I'm sorry," I stammered, suddenly feeling foolish. "I... I heard screams. Is everything okay?"

The woman covered her yawn with a wallet-sized pamphlet

that seemed to have been cut from a magazine or newsletter. It read, "Living with mental illness: A guide to schizophrenia and psychosis." She forced it into my hand and closed the door in my face.

I wanted to believe her, but the screams from inside were too desperate to ignore. I knocked again for reassurance.

When she opened the door a second time, a few rollers were missing from her hair. Her eyes were sharper now, veins poking through, red with exhaustion. "I'm sorry for the noise. She's okay." She handed me another pamphlet. "Read this. It'll all be over soon." She slammed the door again, leaving me in the corridor, clutching the pamphlet with one hand and holding up my shorts with the other.

I read the pamphlet from cover to cover. It only took a few minutes. But the girl inside continued to scream, her voice echoing in my mind, reminding me of Sage. I'd been too afraid to visit him, too ashamed to face Margie again, so I chose to stay away. I wondered what else the old woman could tell me, so I knocked on the door a third time.

When she answered, she was out of breath, more rollers missing from her head, like she'd been in a fight. She tried to hand me another pamphlet, repeating, "I'm sorry for the noise. She's okay."

I blocked the front door with my foot, a sharp pain shooting through my leg like a jolt of electricity. I cringed, instinctively pulling back, but the girl's screams cut through the air, relentless and piercing. "Stop following me, stop touching me, get off of me," she cried, her voice laced with terror.

Ignoring the throbbing in my foot, I hobbled deeper into the condo, each step a reminder of the pain but also of the urgency to help. The layout of the place was eerily similar to my own, but flipped—everything in opposite corners.

The sound echoed from a room in the back, just past the open living space. Beyond the bedroom door lay a makeshift padded room, a sanctuary of soft walls and scattered pillows that seemed to muffle the world outside. The air was thick with the weight of things unspoken, secrets cushioned by the odd calm that filled the space.

In the center, she sat—a young woman, no more than 20, her arms marked with hieroglyphic tattoos that traced stories only she could decipher. Her purple hair spilled in wild disarray, a testament to the untamed spirit within her.

One earring clung to her right earlobe, the other had abandoned its place, lying on the floor next to a small set of keys. Her wrists were bound by pink fuzzy handcuffs, tethering her to the floor in a way that seemed almost gentle, as if the restraints were meant more for her comfort than restraint.

"What the fuck is this?" I yelled, my voice shaking. I rushed to her side, unlocking the handcuffs with the key.

The girl freed her hands and hugged me, squeezing as hard as Sage had tried to squeeze the life out of me. But her hug felt different—better, somehow. As the older woman watched, she noticed the girl calming down and left us alone.

"You saved me," the girl with purple hair whispered, her voice soft and tired. "You saved me." Tears poured down onto my bare chest. "You saved me."

I sat motionless, as if any shift might shatter the fragile spell cast between us. There was a strange, unfamiliar comfort in the way she nestled against me, as though I had somehow become her sanctuary. A quiet pride swelled within me, a warmth I hadn't anticipated, filling the hollow spaces that years of striving and doing had never touched. I had spent my life chasing after things, seeking validation in places that always left me empty. But here, in this moment, I was valued —truly seen—by someone who needed nothing from me except my presence.

Her trust wrapped around me like a gentle embrace, unspoken but deeply felt, and it awakened something profound within me—a sense of purpose I had never known. It wasn't about being useful or successful; it was about being enough, just as I was. The weight of that realization settled into my bones, bringing with it a quiet, aching joy. I didn't know what I had done to deserve this, but for the first time, I wasn't questioning it. I simply wanted to hold onto it, to let this newfound sense of worth linger a little longer, as if savoring a taste of something I had been starving for my entire life.

Still, doubt gnawed at the edges of my newfound confidence, like a parasite feeding on my nerves. Was it really me she needed, or was it just the lingering scent of that cologne, clinging to me like a ghost? What could a beautiful, tattooed girl—so full of life, chaos, and fire—possibly see in a brother like me? I was nothing special, just a broken man, haunted by too many scars and too few victories. Yet, as I held her, her gaze cut through my insecurities like a knife, making them waver, if only for a moment. In her eyes, I was something more—something strong, unshakable. A titan, even. The weight of her trust pressed down on me, heavy and almost unbearable, yet grounding. But I could feel her body soften against me, her breath slowing, as if in that fleeting moment, I was enough. She drifted into sleep, her fears dissolving into the quiet, and for reasons beyond my understanding, the girl found peace in my arms.

"Have you seen me before?" she asked in a faint whisper.

I didn't answer, just let her rest her head on my chest until she drifted off, her breathing turning into soft snores. I made sure she was deep in her much-needed sleep. I was comfortable too, leaning against the soft walls and floor, holding this fragile woman who trusted me completely. The room, which had once felt like a chamber of torture, now seemed different—almost peaceful.

When I finally slipped out of the padded room, the old woman was wide awake, sitting on the couch, watching the news, drinking her coffee.

"Want some coffee?" she asked, her accent a mix of Out West Chicago and something Asian I couldn't quite place.

"No thanks," I replied, still holding onto my shorts. "Never tried coffee before."

"Aye, uh!" she exclaimed, waving her hand dismissively. "Young man like you, never tried coffee? Come, come. You sit, I pour. We talk."

I followed her into the small kitchen, the smell of strong coffee and something spicy filling the air. She bustled around, pouring me a cup, all the while peering at me with sharp, curious eyes.

"So, you my neighbor, eh? I see you come, go. Always with pretty girls. You some kind of playboy?" She chuckled, but her eyes were serious, assessing.

I shifted uncomfortably under her gaze. "I... uh..."

"Never mind, never mind," she waved her hand again. "I'm Ruth. That girl in there, that's Hope. We work together, night shift at a factory in the south suburbs. Six months we live here now. You know why we move here?"

I shook my head, taking a sip of the strong, bitter coffee.

Ruth leaned in, watched me not enjoy my first sip ever, her voice dropping to a conspiratorial whisper. "Hope, she has… problems. In the head, you know? Her mother, she think devil curse Hope. Can you believe? In this day and age! So Hope, she run away. Pittsburgh. Bad man there, bad drugs. Jail time, even. But she come back, strong girl. We meet at factory, become friends. I help her, she help me. But sometimes, at night…" She trailed off, looking towards the room where Hope slept.

My heart sank. "She still…?"

Ruth nodded, her eyes sad. "Sometimes, she get like that. But she good girl, just need help. Like tonight, you help her. I'm thankful. She's lucky you hear her, lucky you brave." She patted my hand, her grip firm despite her age.

I wasn't sure what to say. The weight of Ruth's words, the truth of Hope's situation, settled heavy on my chest. I thought about Sage again, about all the people I'd used and discarded in my pursuit of something—anything—that would make me feel whole. And here was this girl, broken but strong, fighting demons I couldn't even imagine.

"You take care of her, okay?" Ruth said, her voice firm, pulling me from my thoughts. "She needs someone like you, someone strong."

CHAPTER SEVEN

I kept a safe distance from Hope and her cool friend, Ruth, for what felt like an eternity. They were smart, friendly, and genuine women who deserved peace in their lives, and I had been a magnet for chaos. I didn't want to inflict any harm on them or have them caught in the crossfire of the Marshall family curse, so I made a personal vow to keep my bullshit away. The thought of constantly hiding from two women who lived down the hallway was stressful, but a small price to pay to keep them safe from the dangers of me.

I stayed in the crib most days—watching movies, playing video games, smoking, drinking, and beating my meat. I wasted my life, sitting around feeling sorry for myself, afraid to take my place in the world, not really knowing where to start. When supplies ran low, I'd run out the building from the back entrance, the door hardly anyone used because most folks were afraid of the alley. I'd hit the liquor store for a bottle and a six-pack, shake hands in transaction with the weed guy out front, then hang outside until odd hours when I knew the ladies in unit 7A were likely to miss me. I'd return through the back, tiptoe past their door, not wanting to disturb them or draw attention. Always took the stairs and never responded to phantom knocks at my door. When we locked eyes, I'd wave and keep moving with my face pointed down, then run to my crib and drink until I passed out, or puked. This went on for months.

But then came spring, with its vibrant blooming flowers and warmth. I found myself drawn to its brightness and sounds. The sweet, earthy, woodsy aroma and the promise of fun. My skin came alive. I felt a roaring in my soul that inspired me to get out of hiding, to face the world around me, however it came.

I spent a long afternoon at the park down the street from my building. I began my adventure with a walk on the trail, smoking some flower I'd found in the pocket of an old fall hoodie.

The buzz didn't bring much comfort. There were too many people outside for me to calm my anxious nerves. Cyclists rode too close and fast, people walked large dogs without leashes, joggers with headphones paid no attention. Some folks were selling stuff, others begging. Crowds aren't for me, so I stayed in shaded, less chaotic areas.

I was actually enjoying myself for the first time in months before I bumped into the largest motherfucker I'd ever seen. Knocked me right on my ass. A giant of a man, at least seven feet one and three hundred twenty pounds. He had a solid fat neck and shoulders as wide as a doorway, biceps bulging through his brown trench coat, and wore a tight Coogi sweater beneath it that looked like it was found in the trash. I scrambled to stand, but he lifted me with ease, using a single hand.

"Aye, man... Watch where you're going!" I yelled, my voice cracking slightly, betraying my attempt at bravado.

"What's the rush?" He laughed away my weak threat while patting my pockets like a cop. "What happened to the smoke that you had?"

My heart raced. I showed my empty hands, trying to keep them from shaking. "How long have you been watching me?" I asked, attempting to walk away.

The man's dirty face twisted in anger. He seemed to black out for a moment, briefly lost in the hell of his mind. Then, as if a light bulb went off, he quickly came back to his senses, maybe realized he didn't want to kill me in public. He wiped the dust off me, using his large sandpaper-like hands to push me off balance, taunting me with his strength, alerting me that one of his arms could match the weight of my body. He saw the fear in my eyes and smiled, stepping closer, blocking my path.

The man wore a face like an angry Kimbo Slice. Even his smile was intimidating. His eyes could've cut me. "What's so special about you?" He asked, spitting a kind of brown shit next to my shoes, like he'd been chewing tobacco. I felt his burning hot breath on my face. Spray from his spit hit my hand on its way to the ground.

Hunched over me, blocking out the sun while I shrank in his shadow, he placed his heavy hands on my shoulders; the weight holding me down. I looked around desperately for help, but no one seemed to notice or care as his hands added pressure that weakened my knees and shortened my breath. I thought to punch him, or kick him in the nuts and running back home but was too scared to move.

The man also seemed distracted, looking over my shoulders a few times, maybe scoping for witnesses or expecting a friend. I felt like a worm on a hook. The fear provided enough adrenaline for me to shake myself away. I dodged him when he tried to reclaim me, then fast-walked smoothly towards the chess players, hoping their presence would be my salvation.

The giant man became a shadow, felt him breathing down my neck as I tried to ignore him. I feared him punching the back of my head, drilling my head into the ground with only one of his hands and the same jeering smile on his face but I couldn't turn around to look back and see it coming. It was a 10 yard walk that felt more like a mile. I picked up the pace of my steps. Flopped down at the first open table I reached, across from a kid who awaited a challenge.

Scared, shamed, and weakened by an awkward encounter. I couldn't believe how afraid I was. My hands were pulsating, had a shortness of breath, and my heart felt hollow, like it couldn't find a rhythm to beat to. I looked around, slowly and carefully, still feeling the large man's shadow behind me, but he wasn't there. The large angry man had gone.

I stayed around the chessmen for a while, just to be safe. Joined the many chess players who lined the games up in

SHAUNN NORTHERN

rows of black and white roll-up mats. I lost every match. Moved from one bench to the next, lost a few extra dollars and more confidence. The mental ass-kicking I received playing chess was equivalent to the physical one I would have gotten by that big, angry, homeless motherfucker. I had to go, but first, checked every direction to make sure the path was safe and free.

My heart was still racing, palms sweaty, as I scanned the park. The encounter with the giant man had left me shaken, more aware than ever of my vulnerability. It was as if the world had suddenly become a more dangerous place, filled with unpredictable threats. I felt exposed, naked almost, without the false confidence the cologne had once given me. This was the real me—scared, unsure, always on the defensive.

Then, Hope springs, when I least expected her to. She was standing in front of an easel near a large sitting rock and a tree, wearing a smock around her waist, with many different

84

colored pencils, colored chalk, scissors, and other mediums that stuck out the pockets. She was drawing a couple who posed patient and still for their masterpiece. Hope had entered a zone, smiling hard like she'd been listening to God. I couldn't look away.

Hope had changed her hair color from purple to black. Beneath her smock, running pants and a sports top that showed off her stomach, like she'd run a marathon or had a workout before she went there to paint.

She must've felt me watching. Women's intuition, I guess. Turned and looked directly at me, no one else. Didn't miss. Her face lit up with recognition, a smile spreading across her features. She jumped up and down, waving me over enthusiastically. I couldn't fight it. I got closer, reluctantly dragging my feet, so she ran towards me and hugged me, leaving her customers stuck in their pose.

"Hello, my hero," she said, her voice warm and welcoming.

"I'm nobody's hero," I mumbled, looking down at my shoes.

"Boy, please!" She pushed me away playfully, laughing. "Why have you been hiding from us?"

"Hiding? I..."

"Don't lie," she interrupted, rolling her eyes while maintaining her smile.

I exhaled the long breath I'd been holding. "It's better for you if I just stayed out of the way."

"Why?"

"Because, trouble follows me everywhere I go. I'm cursed."

Hope laughed hard, an ugly wail that made her hold her stomach. The sweet-looking couple she'd been drawing grew tired of waiting, took their sketch, and left without paying. Hope waved them goodbye, wiping tears from her eyes.

That shit was embarrassing. I hadn't been laughed at like that since I lived with the Russell's. I turned to walk away, but

Hope stopped me. She grasped my arm, her touch gentle but firm. Her eyes met mine, filled with concern and something else I couldn't place.

"Please stay. Please, stop running away," she said softly, her hand resting on her chest.

She refused to let go of my arm. I stared back into her face. Her eyes were dark honey brown, but one had violet-colored strikes, like a marble. Heterochromia. The room had been too dark for me to notice on our first encounter.

Felt like I should've said something smart and impressive. I wanted to tell her something cool about me, but couldn't think of anything worth sharing. She was an artist, had been to jail, gets to have some cool-ass delusions every once in a while, and there I was, a confused, depressed, nameless misfit, with 21 years of nothing done on this earth, on his way to being an alcoholic, womanizing, coward who gets punked and bullied by random bums in the park. I Wasn't used to anyone being nice to me, respecting me, not since Sergeant

Wilson. Not without the cologne.

The girl could sense by then that I was off. Instead of sending me away, or clowning me more for being pitiful and insecure, she asked, "Can I draw you?"

Hope ripped a page from her drawing pad and broke out a fresh canvas. Pointed to the large sitting rock and told me to prepare my most comfortable pose.

"I never really had the chance to thank you." She said.

"You thanked me plenty times, enough already."

"You don't understand, I had been having that terrible nightmare, over and over, for months. I am attacked by a man —my ex boyfriend. He finds me in my dreams, does horrible things to me. I'm kicking him, punching him, biting him, but he can't feel me. He never stops. I'm screaming in that dream, but no one can hear me." Hope took a deep breath. She's crying, but she let her tears fall down without wiping her face, like she wasn't ashamed of her emotions. I'd never seen it before. "Sometimes, in my dream, he rips my clothes off, throws me on the concrete, and takes whatever he wants from my body."

Hope lifted her head around the easel, to see if I was listening. I didn't know the words to say, so I nodded.

"I first had the nightmare when I moved back to Chicago." She said with a sniffle. "Had the same dream again a few months later. Thought I saw him in real life one day, watching me from a distance. I ran all the way home from where I was. Took a cut through the park, a bus out of the way, just to make sure he didn't follow and see where I lived. The dreams started happening more frequent after that, from once or twice a month to a few times a week. But I haven't had that nightmare since the night you came and saved me."

Her words sent a chill down my spine. The way she described her ex-boyfriend, the fear in her voice—it reminded me of the giant man in the park, how I backed down and folded like a sucker.

"I was dreaming that same damned dream: My ex

boyfriend, broke into my house, grabbed me, and punched me to the ground, stuffed drugs down my throat. But that last time, you were there. You broke through the door like the feds and scared the man away. It was you. You were there in my dream, then I woke up and saw you, for real. In person. I saw your face as clear as day. You were there." Hope looked to me, for some kind of explanation. Asked, "How is that possible?"

I listened to her, trying to piece together her words with a mix of concern and confusion. I wanted to believe her, but schizophrenia was something I knew next to nothing about. How do you respond to something like that? The rational part of my brain wanted to dismiss it as a coincidence, but after everything I'd experienced with the cologne and my family history, could I really be sure?

"Wow, Hope," I started, a slight scratch in my voice. "That's... that's intense. I mean, dreams can be so vivid, right? And sometimes, they just feel so real. Like, I had this dream once where I was flying over the city, and it felt like I could actually feel the wind on my face. Crazy, huh?"

She looked at me again, her eyes searching for something more, then returned to her drawing. Said, "I think he does it on purpose."

"Does what?" He, who?"

"My ex. He's so mean, I think he found a way to stalk my dreams."

"You mean, like Freddy Kruger?" I smirked, then immediately regretted it.

I waited for her laugh, a giggle, or a smirk that never came. Realized that she was serious. "The beautiful ones are always a little crazy," I thought to myself. But then I remembered Sage, his warnings about curses and his violent reaction to me. Who was I to judge what was possible?

"You know, Hope," I began, choosing my words carefully, "I don't know much about dreams or... or the kind of things you're describing. But I do know that what you're feeling is real. The fear, the anxiety—that's all real. And maybe... maybe there's more to it than I understand. I mean, my family has its own history of strange stuff happening. So, I guess what I'm saying is, I might not get it all, but I believe that you believe it. And that's what matters, right?"

Hope's gaze softened, a small smile tugging at the corners of her mouth. "You really mean that?"

I nodded, surprised to find that I did mean it. "Yeah, I do. And hey, the important thing is, you're safe now. And if being there in your dream helped somehow, then I'm glad. Even if I don't understand how it happened."

Hope had stopped drawing, her full attention on me now. "You know, Walter, you're different from most people. Most would just think I'm crazy."

"Well, maybe we're all a little crazy," I said with a shrug. "I mean, look at me—I spent months hiding from the nicest neighbors I've ever had because I thought I was cursed."

That got a laugh out of her, a genuine one this time. She

returned to her drawing, a comfortable silence falling between us. As I watched her work, I felt something shift inside me. Maybe I didn't have all the answers, maybe the world was stranger and more dangerous than I knew, but sitting here with Hope, I felt... okay. For the first time in a long time, I felt like maybe I could face whatever came next.

Hope lifted the canvas off the easel, held it at the length of her arms and smiled with great pride at her work. She turned it around and showed me her masterpiece.

I didn't recognize the man in the picture. She'd drawn a man with a serious, sparkling smile, intelligent eyes, standing confidently, holding a sword of honor. It wasn't a cartoon caricature, but a real, true-to-life sketch of my face, drawn with charcoal and chalk. I couldn't believe what I saw. Stood there, stunned, unable to process. Part of me wanted to see myself the way she seemed to see me. I just didn't. I simply couldn't.

Hope's cheeks were madly flushed when she glanced

between me and the drawing. She bit her lower lip, her eyes squinting, shining with a mix of shyness and admiration. "You know what, Walter?" she said softly, her voice barely a whisper. "You're pretty handsome."

CHAPTER EIGHT

I spent a few more hours in the park with Hope, mesmerized by her charm, wit, and corny sense of humor. The way her eyes lit up when she spoke of her art almost inspired me to get up and paint. Despite all she'd been through, she remained soft, undeniably feminine, with a delicate strength that took my breath away.

As the sun began to set, casting a golden glow over the park, I found myself drawn to Hope in a way I'd never experienced before. Her laughter, melodic and genuine, sent shivers down my spine. The way she tucked a strand of hair behind her ear, the gentle curve of her neck, the warmth of her hand when it accidentally brushed against mine—every little detail seemed magnified, electrifying.

She listened to me, really listened, her eyes following my mouth as I spoke. She never interrupted, just hung onto my words, making me feel like a scholar instead of a man who'd lost his way, or never had one to begin with. It made me want to hold her, protect her, to give her what she needed to ensure she might stay as she was.

As twilight deepened, our conversation took on a more intimate tone. Hope's eyes, illuminated by the soft glow of the park lamps, seemed to hold secrets I longed to uncover. Without realizing it, we had moved closer, our bodies almost touching.

"Walter," she whispered, her breath warm against my cheek, "I feel so safe with you."

My heart raced as I gently cupped her face in my hands. Time seemed to stand still as our lips met, soft and tentative at first, then with growing passion. The world around us faded away, leaving only the two of us, wrapped in each other's arms under the starry sky.

What followed was a beautiful, tender exploration of each other. Our bodies moved together in perfect harmony, hidden in the shadows of a secluded corner of the park. It was more than just physical; it was a connection of souls, a moment of pure, unbridled intimacy that left us both breathless and changed.

Afterwards, as we lay on the grass, Hope's head resting on my chest, I told her things that night I hadn't even whispered to myself. We connected in a way that felt like destiny had a hand in it. Amazing. I'd gone out to play in the sun feeling depressed and came home inspired. I noticed how filthy and disorganized my condo had gotten. Stayed up late, throwing away all the empty and half-full cognac bottles, taking out the garbage, cleaning the bathroom and kitchen while listening to some Wu-Tang, Pete Rock, and Nas.

I woke up the next morning thinking of the woman whose name was the only thing stronger than fear. I could've jumped right out of bed and run to 7A. For the first time since they moved into the building, I was happy she lived down the hall.

So, I called her. Ruth answered the house phone; I heard Hope blushing in the background when Ruth called out for her.

"Hope, your savior's on the phone."

"What?"

"It's that skinny boy from down the hall who doesn't like coffee. You know, the male prostitute."

Ruth returned to the phone. "Here she comes, skinny boy."

"Thanks."

"What you doing over there? No clients today?"

"I'm not a prostitute, Ruth. Women just like me." I laughed, not really sure if I was lying or not.

Hope snatched the phone from Ruth. I could hear their muffled noises, scratches, and giggles. There was a tickle-fight over the phone, and Hope won. She jumped on the receiver, breathless, using a joke to break the ice.

"Well, damn, just saw you last night. Hooked already?" She

laughed with pride.

"Yep. I can't deny it. I actually called to invite you to breakfast. Best way to top off that great night of talking and bonding. You down?"

"I'm not really hungry," she said. "But I'll go and watch you eat and talk your ear off some more."

"Well, it's on then."

"I can get ready in 25 minutes."

I hung up the phone. Tried to play it cool, but she might've heard my shout from down the hall. I threw my fists in the air, blasted music, and danced all the way to the bathroom.

Standing in front of the mirror, I brushed my teeth while butchering the lyrics to "Bonita Applebum," rocking my head to the vibe of the song. I splashed a little slobber on the sink and realized how ridiculous I looked with thick white paste dripping off my mouth. Rinsing, I noticed the scar on my chin from when I was 15, climbing a steel-wired fence. I saw the bags beneath my eyes from nights of no sleep, how I desperately needed my hair combed out or cut. My eyes were too close together, my ears kind of pointy, and my bottom tooth had a small chip in front.

As I stared at my reflection, a creeping doubt began to gnaw at the edges of my excitement. Hope was absolutely stunning. Her last man probably had baby-soft skin, large muscles, and a Louisville Slugger in his pants. I didn't have all that. I wasn't a tough guy or a rebel. I wasn't a party guy who frequented nightclubs and knew all the latest dance moves. I wasn't enterprising, didn't have connections, didn't like too many people at all.

Truth was, I was barely six feet, 190 pounds soaking wet, with no family, no credit, no job, and no purpose. I didn't know how long my money would last, or how to fix a house, or how to treat a woman I actually liked. I thought there was too much wrong for everything to go right. I put my head down again.

Opening the cabinet door to return the toothpaste, I saw

the damn cologne sitting right on the shelf. I picked it up in disbelief, thinking about wearing it. It felt cold, like it had sat in a fridge overnight. Other bottles were room temperature, so I tossed the cologne in the trash by the sink.

I picked out fresh clothes and laid them on the bed. Trying on the pants, I felt a bulge in the pocket. It was the same damned vial of cologne. I grabbed a permanent marker from my desk and wrote "Go away" on the bottle. Opening the bedroom window, I tossed it out and danced to the sound of it shattering on the ground, almost in the same spot as before.

Fully dressed, I went to the kitchen and opened the fridge for a bottle of water. Behind it, you guessed it, was that same damned vial of cologne with "Go away" faintly marked on the side, as if the words had been written years ago. This time, I didn't move the bottle. I slammed the fridge door and left my apartment in a fit.

Determined to enjoy myself, I got my nerves together and went down to 7A. Ruth told me Hope would meet me downstairs and that she was working hard to look her best for our date. I said, "Cool! But tell Hope she's already pretty enough."

I made my way to the parking lot, fired up the Caddy, and pulled around to the lobby doors, parking at the curb. I flipped on the hazard lights, let the top down, and blasted the local jazz station I usually tuned in for late-night joy rides on Lake Shore Drive.

As I waited for Hope, I felt a bead of sweat trickle down my temple. My hands, resting on the steering wheel, felt clammy. I wiped them on my jeans, noticing how my palms left damp marks on the denim. My heart began to race, its rhythm slightly off, like a drummer losing his beat.

Hope came out looking fine as a brand new day. She wore an all-purpose dress she likely had to roll down her body, sunglasses, and comfortable walking shoes. The sight of her took my breath away, just as it had the night before in the park. The memory of our intimate moment flashed through my mind, sending a shiver down my spine. But with it came a wave of doubt. How could someone so beautiful, so full of life, want someone like me?

I looked down at myself, wondering if I was fresh enough for her, hoping my money and jokes would be enough. I froze. Didn't try to open her car door or stand on the curb like a gentleman. Everything felt off and I didn't know why.

As Hope got closer to the car, my armpits, neck, and nose started sweating profusely. A cold dread crept up my spine, each vertebra feeling like an ice cube stacked on top of another. My fingers trembled on the steering wheel, and a familiar emptiness gnawed at my gut. The world around me seemed to blur at the edges, Hope's approaching figure the only thing in clear focus.

Suddenly, the glove box sprang open, like it was pushed by an unseen hand. There it was again—the God damned cologne, rolling onto the floor mat, the words "Go away" still faintly visible on its surface.

The sight of it, like a sucker punch. My vision narrowed. Sweat continued to trickle down my back, my shirt clinging uncomfortably to my skin. My chest tightened, each breath becoming a labored gasp. The voice in my head, the one that always told me I wasn't good enough, roared to life, drowning out everything else.

Hope's innocence radiated as she reached for the door handle, unaware of the turmoil raging inside me. In that moment, she seemed too pure, too good for someone like me. The weight of my fears, my inadequacies, and my cursed legacy crashed down on me all at once. I couldn't do it. I couldn't taint her with my chaos.

Before I could second-guess myself, I slammed the car into drive and peeled away from the curb. The girl of my dreams, left standing alone on the sidewalk because I was too much of a pussy to face my own demons.

CHAPTER NINE

When I'm set inside the flow of the streets, I can ease into a state of meditation. The gentle hum of the engine, hand vibrating on the steering wheel, and the panoramic scenes of the city passing by create a soothe that I can only get when out on the road.

I drove around the whole damned day. Pushed the Caddy up north, as far as Evanston, then went south, all the way to Kankakee. Burned a full tank of gas in a foolish attempt to run from myself.

Returned to my neighborhood around 4 p.m. and landed in the parking lot of the 63rd Street Beach. The atmosphere was lively, with everyone seemingly outside and enjoying themselves. Their laughter felt directed at me, like they played and had a ball with their loved ones to taunt me. I stayed and watched closer. Honed in on the pain and the pity that I held for myself. I deserved to be punished, teased, and made to look like a fool for leaving Hope standing outside on the curb.

My mind raced. A brainstorm of doubt. Wondered how I could sneak into my building without being seen and avoid any further embarrassment. And then, as fate would have it, the cologne rolled out on the floor from underneath the passenger seat. I walked the stubborn bottle to the shoreline, hurled it out as far as my muscles allowed and watched it splash into Lake Michigan. Yet, my return to the car revealed its unwelcome reappearance right there on the seat. For the first time in my life, I was faced with a problem that I couldn't run away from.

Sometimes, when I'm in trouble, afraid, or simply don't know what to do, I close my eyes and speak out to God. With my hands folded tightly together, I promised God I'd become a better man, and apologized to him for my past mistakes. Told God I'd straighten up and fly right if he would grant me a clue. Told him I'd talk to him more, not just on the bad days, and promised that I'd find a church to frequent if he'd only leave a sign of how to vanquish my curse. I really did want to change, do right by people, live the life of a good man, only, I didn't believe that I was capable of being that guy. Wasn't sure if I knew how to be a good man. I was another product of Cadillac Slim, grandson of a pimp. I was the son of a mother who rebelled against her Pastor Rev. Dr. Father, who got involved with two brothers and tore a family apart. I was possibly the son of a man who killed his brother, or the son of the brother who was killed. I didn't think I had it in me to be a good man, so I prayed with half-a-heart.

Wilson once told me, "Prayer without works is dead." He cursed me out a lot, but he read that bible just as much. I guess he meant well. So after praying, I opened my eyes and went to work, searching for God's answer. Started in the glove box. Found liquor store receipts, old parking tickets, coupons, expired registrations, and night-club ticket stubs. Not a clue about the sweaty cologne or how to get rid of it.

Checked the trunk. Found a stack of I.D. Cards from various states: Illinois, California, Nevada, Florida, New York, and Texas. Each card a different name, yet the same corny photo of Slim wearing square reading glasses and a black bow tie. Also found a rusty old pistol, a switchblade, dull book of matches, a can of lighter fluid, some old-ass rags, and a tome wrapped in a bag sealed with duct tape.

The blade was still sharp, cut through the tape like a hot knife through butter and unraveled a scrapbook of pictures, a bunch of random phone numbers, and newspaper clippings. Read a few headlines of Slim's colorful history—petty thefts, a house fire, and a daring local bank heist. There were very few photos of Sage, none of Melvin, or Laura.

The predominant figure in the photos, however, was Slim himself, surrounded by a bevy of women usually dressed like he and Don "Magic" Juan had shopped the same tailor. To my surprise, the women seemed happy, even proud to be around such a horrible man. One photo, in particular, stood out—a photo of Slim and a much younger woman, standing on 47th Street in Bronzeville, in front of a store called "Nona's". I'd been there before, stopped in there to grab a couple dozen roses. Decided right then that it was time to go back.

With the scrapbook's revelations fresh in my mind, I steered the Caddy towards Bronzeville. The streets seemed to guide me, as if Slim's ghost was at the wheel. Before long, I found myself parked in front of Nona's, the flower shop from the photo. Taking a deep breath, I stepped out of the car and pushed open the shop's door, a small bell announcing my arrival.

I was the only customer inside Nona's haven of flowers, plants, and herbs. Fresh blooms adorned the shelves, counters, inside a few pots on the floor, and hanging from the ceiling. The air, saturated with the fragrance of each blossom, was like standing in a women's perfume shop.

"How I can help you, chéri? Buyin' flowers for a femme or a ti fi?" The woman's Creole accent was thick and melodious.

"Are you Nona?" I asked, getting straight to the point.

The woman smiled, exposing her beautiful teeth. She glanced at my shoes, held up my arm and dangled it to test out the weight. Stated, "You look too young to be a gendarme," she laughed, "Oui, I'm Nona, de Plant Priestess, de Herb Witch, de Botanical Healer, Floral Shaman of de Chi; in de flesh."

Nona's afro was a striking, vibrant gray, and her skin displayed a clear peanut butter brown. A network of wrinkles on her face suggested she was well in her 70's, yet the curves and firmness of her body made me doubt it. Purple reading glasses. Black smock with dirty hand prints protected the yellow dress with white flowers she wore.

"Do you remember this man?" I asked. Pulled out the picture of Nona and my grandfather standing outside of her store.

Nona blushed, seizing the photo to fan off her flashbacks of Slim. "Cadillac Slim," she giggled. "De Englewood Casanova…"

Nona dreamed at the photo like a delighted schoolgirl. Pressed her glasses on her nose to make sure she was seeing things clearly.

"Where you find dis picture, bébé?"

"A pig gave it to me," I grunted.

Nona's eyes lit up, a spark of recognition flashing across her face. She shifted closer, her scent a mixture of flowers and Jean Naté.

"You Slim's boy, ain't you?" she asked, her voice warm with recognition. "I should've known. You got his eyes, his stance."

I nodded, unsure how to respond.

"Well, let me tell you somethin', chéri," Nona continued, her voice dropping to a conspiratorial whisper. "I was one of Slim's women, you know. One of his favorites. In fact, I'm his baby mama. Got a grandson from him too."

My eyes widened at this revelation. "You're... you're my grandfather's..."

"Dat's right, bébé," Nona nodded, a mixture of pride and something else in her eyes. "Which makes you and my Killer cousins. Family."

Before I could process this information, Nona was suddenly behind me. Eased on in there like a pro, her old wrinkled hands found their place on my shoulders, began kneading my muscles in a firm, circular motion.

"Now, tell Nona," she purred, "what else did dey give you from Slim?"

"Uh, his car, and some other stuff," I mumbled, uncomfortable with her sudden closeness.

Nona's demeanor shifted instantly. Her hands tightened on my shoulders, nails digging in slightly. "His car? What else?" Her voice had lost its warmth, replaced by a sharp edge.

"N-Nothing," I lied, unsure of her sudden change. "Just

some old junk."

"Don't lie to Nona, chéri," she hissed, her hands moving to my neck. I felt the icy touch of tiny razor-sharp blades pressing tight to my skin. "What else did dey give you?"

"I don't have anything," I strained to say. Began to empty my pockets to prove it. My wallet, keys, blade, and that relentless cologne bottle, tossed it all on the floor.

Nona recognized the cologne immediately. The bottle fell to the floor without breaking or cracking, and she dove across the counter like a bomb had gone off. "Get it out of here," she cried.

I wiped the blood from my neck, checking the small wounds, made sure I was cool. Then I picked up the bottle of cologne, begged her.

"Please! I need your help! This cologne... It's stalking me. I can't get rid of it."

I fumbled the bottle in my hands and it fell to the floor again. Nona screamed like a banshee. I didn't understand the

113

dangers of it. I watched it fall without breaking, kicked it over where Nona continued to lay on the ground, using a potting table for a bunker.

Nona snapped. Her eyes had gone dim to a dilated grim in her gaze. Both brows raised, with tears that seemed hesitant to fall as she hysterically ran from the bottle, throwing pots and garden tools in its direction. "Killer!" She called for reinforcements. "Killer, help me, I'll do anyt'ing!"

I took a knee. Hid behind a row of white orchids while I gathered my wallet and keys.

"Who is Killer?"

Nona, fueled by fear, continued throwing flower pots, scissors, bags of dirt in my row, hoping one would knock me out.

The back door to the shop slammed open, and the heavy, crunching footsteps of large shoes entered the room. "What's de emergency?" A dark, smoky voice inquired. A cold familiar tone that often comes with years of pain combined with the low and raspy monotone pitch of resentment.

My blood ran cold as I recognized that voice. It was the same one that had sent a chill down my spine at the park the day before. The voice of the very large bully who had threatened me. And now, I realized with a jolt, my cousin.

"Killer, it's him! Slim's boy!" Nona cried out, her voice a mix of fear and anger. "He's got de cologne!"

Staying hidden, I sat upright and stealthily crawled towards the front of the store. Moving from one table to the next while the large man, Killer - my cousin - looked in every other direction. He seemed happy to find me. Charged at me, knocking over a table of flowers. I barely made it out the door, jumped to the sidewalk like the building was burning. Never looked back.

I got home after 8, but waited hours for the building to calm before I entered. Faint screams echoed from the elevator, and as I approached my apartment, Hope's voice grew clearer. "No! Leave me alone! Get off of me!" Ruth had left a stack of pamphlets for the tenants, hanging from a box on her door—a clear sign that Hope's nightmares had returned.

I staggered down the hall, a long walk of shame to my condo, enveloped by Hope's continuous screams, cries, and calls for help. They wrapped around me like a suffocating blanket. I prayed for the strength to crash through Hope's door and save her like I had in the fall. My hand trembled as it reached for the doorknob. I tightened my fist, ready to bang on the door and apologize. My body tensed, prepared to spring into action, to be the hero she once saw in me. But the memory of my earlier failure—of driving away and leaving her stranded—paralyzed me. The fear of disappointing her again, of not being the man she deserved, rooted me to the spot. I wanted to break down the door, to swoop her off her feet so she could maybe have a good night's rest. I could have saved her again, so that she could save me. Again, I was too much of a pussy to do it.

CHAPTER TEN

I didn't wake until the next afternoon. The first thing that caught my eye was the bottle of cologne perched on my dresser, its presence a mocking reminder of my failure. I didn't bother trying to break it or toss it aside; that would have required more energy than I could muster. Instead, I dragged myself out of the tangled mess of sheets, stumbled to the edge of the bed, and emptied my stomach into the garbage can by my nightstand.

As the heaving subsided, I glanced around the room and took in the aftermath of last night's breakdown. The chaos was a direct result of the torment I'd endured—listening to Hope's screams and cries from down the hallway, her pain echoing through my mind until I lost control. Fueled by desperation and frustration, I'd torn the place apart in a fit of rage. Now, the thought of facing the day brought a pounding headache and a wave of regret, each throb a painful reminder of the mess I'd made and the helplessness I felt.

Life didn't seem worth the trouble. I thought about ending it all right then and there. Picked up that old rusty pistol I'd found in the Caddy, put the barrel in my mouth, then next to my ear, and on the side of my head. Couldn't find the guts to pull the trigger. Minutes later, I raised the blade to my throat. Couldn't finish that either.

I grabbed what was left of a wasted cognac bottle, gulped the last of it, then dragged myself towards the kitchen in the back of my crib wearing basketball shorts, a beater, and a lone black sock that helped carry the mood. Opening my back window, I pushed out the screen and looked downward at the ground to see how far I could fall. My tears dropped down to the concrete. I envied the splash.

The water pouring from my eyes challenged my vision, but

I could hear the sounds of life outside that window—dogs barking, cars honking, sirens wailing in the distance, a jackhammer breaking the pavement. People were engaged in the rhythm of life. The vibe was more alive than I wanted to be.

As I stood there, contemplating the futility of it all, a flicker of movement in the alley below caught my eye. I wiped the tears away, blinking to clear my vision. That's when I saw him—the man Nona called "Killer," who had threatened to end me. He was lurking in the corners, navigating the shadows across the alley from my building, seemingly searching for a way to sneak inside.

I quickly sat on the floor of my kitchen. Thoughts raced— how in the hell did he know where to find me? Darker thoughts followed—maybe he had come there to kill me?

Without hesitation, I threw on my joggers and gym shoes, then slipped out the back door to meet with my doom. Found Killer in the parking lot, scoping out the cars, likely trying his best to find the Caddy.

I set my jaw, narrowed my eyes, and clenched my fists so tight my knuckles turned white. Shifting into a southpaw stance, I prepared for what might be my last stand. It was going to be a soldier's death for me.

"Looking for me, Motherfucker?" I hurled my words at him, hoping to incite a response that would bring out his worst, but Killer turned and laughed in my face.

"Calm down, li'l man," he said, his Creole accent thick and syrupy.

"Little?" The word hung in the air as I charged at Killer. Punched him in his hard stomach several times, my favorite combo, then jumped up to swing at his face, landed one smack in the jaw.

Killer grimaced a bit, but was unfazed by my attack. "I'm disconnected," he said, his demeanor calm. His voice sounded like he hadn't had a drink of water in years.

"What you talkin' 'bout, disconnected? Disconnected from

what?"

"I don' feel shit."

Killer straightened his dusty trench coat, started wiping off my punches with his hands. "Look, man, I didn' come here to hurt you," he continued. "I have a message from Nona. She wants to help."

Listen: I'm not dumb. Of course I didn't trust that motherfucker. But desperation proved a much more potent persuader. If Nona could offer a chance for me to break the family curse, then maybe I had a chance at living a free life. Hearing him out was a risk that I couldn't ignore. Plus, he was family, right? Aren't you supposed to trust family? The concept was so foreign to me, I didn't know how to navigate it.

"Help me, how?" I asked, my voice a mix of suspicion and hope.

"She wants to meet you at de shop tomorrow mornin'... said to bring de sweaty cologne and Slim's old picture book."

The mention of Slim's picture book, a detail I had yet to disclose, was a clue that Nona shared a closeness with Slim.

"Sweaty Cologne," I mused, "the name fits."

"Nothin' is funny. Dat's some dangerous shit."

I pulled the bottle from my pocket, knew it would be there. Presented it like a Golden Globe Award. "What? This stuff?"

Killer took it back like the Cha-Cha Slide. Almost jumped out of his Freddy Krueger sweater. The man had his hands up, mouth cracked, and eyes bulged wide like his life had flashed before them. He'd finally lost his cool. Said something like, "Keep dat bullshit out of my face!"

"You scared, Killer?" I asked.

"My name's not Killer," he responded. Extended his hand to proposition a truce. "My name is Nazaire M. Lacoste, but you should call me Naz."

I extended my hand to help Killer up, but it was like trying to lift a boulder. His massive frame—all 7 feet and 320-plus pounds of athletic muscle - barely budged as I strained, my own 5'11", 190-pound frame feeling puny in comparison. When he finally got to his feet, I felt a fleeting moment of strength, remembering how he'd knocked me down in the park. It felt good to dish it back, but the satisfaction was hollow. I owed this small victory to the sweaty cologne, not my own prowess.

I accepted Naz's hand. Asked, "Like the rapper?"

Naz grinned. Confirmed, "Like de rapper."

I positioned myself to lean against the trunk of a burgundy Chevy Caprice, maintaining enough distance to hear Naz clearly but stay out of his reach. When Naz joined me, sitting on the opposite side of the Chevy, his weight caused the shocks to squeal and the front end of the car to rise slightly.

I told him, "I heard Nona call you Killer, back at the shop."

"Nona's my mère. She can call me what she wants."

Naz's face softened, a hint of vulnerability creeping into his usually stoic expression. "Look, I ain't proud of it, but I gave her a hard time growin' up. Single mom, you know? My dad has been in jail since I was born, but Nona stepped up, did the best she could for me before I left and came back... Now I'm just tryin' to make it up to her, be de son she deserves."

He raised his battered hands, staring at them the same way I stared at the sweaty cologne - like they were a curse he couldn't escape. "I used to be a fighter. Dese fists left a trail of broken faces and concussions in de world of boxin'. My fans used to praise me for how hard I could hit." Naz paused, as if the memory hurt to rekindle. "I was 18-0. Broke 9 jaws, caused 1 seizure. Dey called me Killer Naz."

"So, why the long face? Sounds like something you should be proud of," I interrupted.

Naz scoffed at my ignorance. Looked into the cloudy sky like he was watching a movie. "Cheers can only last for a minute," he continued, his voice heavy with regret. "Cheers turn to boos de very second you lose."

"You lost a fight? To a human?" I smirked, trying to lighten the mood, but Naz didn't budge. Instead, he decided to go a little deeper and drop the bomb on me.

"A man died in de ring, yeah," Naz said, his Creole accent thickening with emotion. "Dat motherfucker talked all dat shit, but couldn't take a hit. Now, de whole boxin' world hates me for de same damned reason dey used to praise me. I was banned from de sport and locked away for a year. Lost my girl, my money, my career, and my life. Nona was de only person who stuck by me. She still calls me Killer to remind me of what I'm s'posed to do when I get my life right."

As Naz spoke, I found myself torn between sympathy and suspicion. Here was a man who had experienced loss, who understood what it meant to be cursed by your own actions. In a way, we weren't so different. But the memory of his threat in the park still lingered, making it hard to fully trust him. Still, he was family—the only family I had right now. Wasn't I supposed to give him a chance?

Naz never looked me in the eye when he talked. He didn't

once make me feel like he was someone to trust. Despite the familiar nature of avoidance, and the way my skin crawled when he lowered his voice, I was desperate. I had to see Nona and learn what she knows about Slim and the curse.

"Nona knows a lot about nature," Naz continued, his eyes darting around the alley. "Uses herbs, crystals, and stones when she helps people. She can make a tea dat makes liars tell de truth. Reverend Parker says it's witchcraft. Most people t'ink she's a witch, but she's not."

As Naz spoke, I noticed something odd. He began to mirror my posture, subtly at first, then more obviously. When I shifted my weight, he did too. When I crossed my arms, his followed suit. It was unsettling, but I couldn't quite put my finger on why. Even stranger, I realized his accent seemed to be fading, becoming less pronounced with each sentence.

"Does she know a lot about the cologne?" I asked.

"Does she know a lot about de cologne?" Naz repeated, his voice eerily similar to mine.

I frowned, uncomfortable with his mimicry. Naz stood up from the car, the shocks squealing in relief. Then, bizarrely, he returned to a sitting position, moving his body around until he sat in the exact same pose as me, mirroring my stance and mannerisms.

"She's the one who made it," Naz said, his thick Creole accent almost entirely gone now. "Gave it to your grandfather as a gift. She said he intentionally used it the wrong way and now it's gone out of control."

"This is all Slim's fault!" I said, my voice rising with anger.

"This is all Slim's fault!" Naz echoed, sounding exactly like me. He didn't laugh or smirk to show he was teasing.

"Stop doing that!" I snapped, unnerved by his behavior.

"Relax, man. I'm just fucking with you," Naz responded, forcing out a sarcastic laugh.

I brushed off the disrespect, determined to get more information.

"Yeah, fuck Slim," Naz agreed, reverting to his own voice.

"He did Nona dirty. Owes us thousands of dollars."

With my head tilted, I asked, "So, that's why Nona wants to help me, for money?"

Naz paused, his eyes fixed on some distant memory, or idea. "No. That's why I want to help you. Between me and you, this shit is gonna cost you. Nona, on the other hand, she just wants to make things right. She feels responsible."

"How much is this gonna cost me?" I asked, suspicion creeping into my voice.

"How much is dis gonna cost me?" Naz laughed, mimicking me again.

The air between us thickened with uncertainty. Nona, that fit old manipulative seductress in granny panties and blades on her rings, the woman who threatened to slice both my neck and my penis, helping me? I just didn't see it. But I was feeling suicidal as well. Figured I had nothing to lose. "What's the catch?" I asked.

"Well, Nona says there's a thing you gotta do before you

come back to her shop."

"I'm listening," I insisted, while displaying my most skeptical eye.

"I'm listening," Naz tried to mimic and failed due to a crack in his voice.

"I'm listening," Naz tried again.

"I'm listening." Third time's the charm.

"Fuckin' weirdo," I said beneath my breath.

"Fuckin' weirdo," Naz said loud and clear as he reached into his side pocket and pulled out a vintage wooden vial wrapped inside a Jewel's plastic grocery bag. The vial had enigmatic writings all around it, with symbols that were hard to recognize, and a leather rope. Naz popped the cork and said, "She wants you to drink this cleansing brew, to protect her from you. She don't want you bringing all that bad mojo in her flower shop. It took me hours to clean that up. I'm charging you for that too."

"What the hell is that?" were the hard words I chose to

mask the fear in my heart.

Naz raised the vial to my face. "Here! Smell it, but not too hard. It'll burn all de hair in your nose."

Smelled like a strong mix of turpentine, menthol, and cinnamon dirt. Tears rushed to my eyes. I had to close them. Said, "Awe... hell, no! I'm not drinking... this smells like shit."

"Awe... hell, no!" Naz said. Moved his hands and feet to copy mine. "It's not so bad," he laughed. "I drink it all the time. Watch!"

Naz took a whiff of the contents, turned his nose up and coughed. Said, "One shot for this life, one shot for the next," like reciting a prayer, or spell he worked hard to remember. That cold motherfucker, held up the vial, as if he were toasting to heaven. That evil motherfucker, took a nice big gulp, wiped his mouth, and shook away the rigor in his chest. "Shit!" He said. "It's like a very sour fire inside me."

When I finally accepted the vial and bag in my hand, Naz went into a frenzy. Paced back and forth, staring at me the whole time.

"What are you getting out of this?" I asked.

"What are you getting out of this?" Was his response.

"Is this safe?" I hesitated.

"Is it safe?"

Nothing felt right, but I was numb to that. Tried hard to remember the last time life had felt good and couldn't. The pressure was mounting. Here I was, with a chance to maybe break this curse, to understand my family history. Naz was my cousin, shouldn't I trust him? But everything about this felt wrong. Still, what choice did I have? I was desperate, teetering on the edge of giving up entirely. If this was my one shot at answers, at freedom from the curse, didn't I have to take it?

"Fuck it."

"Fuck it!"

I raised the vial to my lips and paused. Took a look inside.

A strange brew it was. An oily, silvery, watery substance that seemed to defy the laws of nature itself. I poured a dab on my hands to check the texture. It took on a mesmerizing quality, rippling and undulating like the surface of a dark, murky pond.

"DON'T WASTE IT!" Naz yelled, as if standing on the edge of catastrophe. "You gotta say everything I said." Naz said, anxiously. Still pacing back and forth like a madman, eyes bulging out of his head. "Nona told me that. You gotta say it. You gotta say it."

"Is this shit flammable?" I asked. Another foolish attempt to try to laugh away the fear.

"Is this shit flammable?" Naz mocked. That time, sounded like a baby, or a whiny little girl.

The closer the vial came to my lips, the bigger Naz's pupils.

"Shut the fuck up and drink it!" he yelled.

My laughing slowed down to a stop. I took a healthy gulp of air to practice the upcoming swallow. Decided not to test the giant's patience any longer.

"One shot for this life, and one for the next."

It was spicy. Like dirt, paint thinner, and cinnamon mouthwash. My stomach churned, like my guts weren't quite where God had planned them to be. I had to take a proper seat.

Naz rolled a blunt and laughed at my tipsy behavior. My words began to slur, and the parking lot, the rear alleyway of my building, the big green dumpsters, all became a blur.

Intoxicated. Drunk, or high, or both. Couldn't tell. Whatever it was had me out on the ground.

"I cuh fee lit," I slurred. "I cuh fee lit rite now!" Sang that embarrassing song over and over until I passed out to sleep.

That's all I can remember from that day: Naz's fake humility—the way he came into my day, disguised as the person to save me, fooling me to believe he held the cure for my blues.

PART TWO

FINDING WALTER MOSLEY

In many places around the world, the transition from boyhood to manhood is usually marked by a profound rite of passage, offering communal support and encouragement. I've never seen that kind of shit around me.

Yo, the Xhosa tribe in South Africa, for instance. They have a Ulwaluko ceremony involving circumcision and seclusion, followed by a celebration where the entire community acknowledges the boy's new status as a man, and not just to help him get drunk like they do over hear. Similarly, the Maasai people in Kenya and Tanzania celebrate with the Eunoto ceremony, marking a young man's transition from warrior to adult with communal festivities and blessings. That's some cool shit.

In Japan, the Genpuku ceremony historically signified a boy's coming of age, where he would receive adult clothing and a whole new name, one that represents his new responsibilities while also passing on a sense of accomplishment and identity.

Here, we have milestones like high school graduation and turning 21, but these often lack the communal support I've seen work in other cultures. Don't get me wrong, those accomplishments should be celebrated, but those kinds of parties feel isolated, especially when you're from a fast-paced city like Chicago where personal achievement often overshadows collective celebration.

Imagine if we adopted something akin to the Shinbyu ceremony in Myanmar, where boys are temporarily ordained as monks and celebrated for their spiritual and personal growth. Or consider the Quinceañera in Hispanic communities. I know it's traditionally for girls, but it represents a community's recognition of a significant life transition. A community's. We need more like that for the world. We should celebrate each other more, as human beings.

Bringing traditions that encourages us to celebrate each other as a cumminity into American culture could bridge a crucial gap, offering young men like myself the encouragement and celebration they might be missing. We can make our own rites of passage, building a communal celebration that acknowledges struggles, celebrates achievements, and supports young men as they step into adulthood. It's about ensuring that no one feels abandoned, or feels tossed into the woods with the wolves—like me...

CHAPTER ELEVEN

A stubborn, high-pitched ringing sound inside my head rudely introduced the new day. It was like a drill boring into my skull, making it hard to breathe a full breath. Every nerve in my body tingled; my nose and fingertips were as cold as icicles. A desperate, hard gasp saved my life.

My eyelids were sealed shut, a stubborn crust keeping them closed, with a dryness that suggested they could bleed if I rubbed them too hard. They needed moisture, something to soften the gritty barrier. I groped inside the darkness, fingers fumbling through what I suspected was trash, until I found a sticky substance. It didn't have a smell, so I massaged it into my eyes until I felt some relief.

As my eyelids slowly parted, the world came into focus—

a world of rust, rot, and refuse. I was lying in a dumpster, surrounded by a grotesque tableau of urban decay. Torn garbage bags spilled their guts around me—soggy newspapers, half-eaten food crawling with maggots, and shattered glass that glinted dully in the weak light filtering through the cracks of the dumpster lid. The stench hit me like a physical force—a noxious cocktail of spoiled milk, rotting vegetables, and something disturbingly organic that I couldn't quite place.

My senses were slowly returning, along with the emptiness that had followed me since childhood. How many times had I awakened like this, lost and alone, in a half-drunken daze, feeling not like myself? My quest for belonging and identity had always felt like fumbling around in the dark, but this... this was different.

I could barely see, feel, or smell the filthy dumpster I appeared to be in. Caught a faint whiff of garbage, and my mouth still tasted like throw-up, cognac, and that potent-ass solution Naz convinced me to drink. The memory of that vile concoction made my stomach churn—a sickly sweet taste with an undercurrent of something chemical, something that shouldn't be consumed by any living being.

My whole body tingled like a major nerve had snapped, and when the ringing in my ears subsided, the sound of raindrops on a hollow sheet of metal crept into the soundscape. My primary senses were slowly returning. Still, something important was missing.

I sat upright inside the dumpster, curled in the fetal position, hugging my knees. The lid was closed just above my head. It took every ounce of strength for me to swing it off to the side and let the rain fall on my face. In that moment, I felt a connection to every lost soul who'd ever sought cleansing, redemption, a fresh start.

My legs were too heavy to move. If my toes weren't tingling, I would have believed I'd become paraplegic. I had to pull myself up, partially over the edge of the dumpster, then threw my heavy body over the edge. The impact sent shockwaves through my unfamiliar frame, each nerve ending screaming in protest. I collapsed a few feet away from the old Chevy Naz and I had leaned on to chat. Memories of my appointment with Nona flooded back.

Seeking clarity, I crawled closer to the Chevy, my limbs feeling like lead weights dragging through molasses. I caught a glimpse of my reflection in the window, and the world tilted on its axis. The image that stared back at me was Naz's face. From his rusty-looking nose that'd been punched too many times, to his eyes that may have seen a couple layers of hell. It was his entire face and body that reflected from that dirty-ass window of the Chevy Caprice. Should've been mine.

I rubbed more rain into my eyes a little harder, checked the mirror again. The same alien face stared back. I turned to a puddle forming on the cracked pavement, hoping for a different truth. But there it was again—Naz's weathered features rippling in the dirty water.

I stood there, paralyzed by the surreal sight, allowed the rain to wash the rest of my dignity down the drains of Chicago. I had been thrust into a nightmare that I couldn't wake from. My very identity hijacked in the most unsettling way.

The scent of the dumpster continued to cling, a tangible reminder of my newest disgrace. My new body, like a meat suit three or four sizes too big, awkwardly draped around my soul like a cloak. Felt like I could lose it any minute. And it itched, consistently. I scratched myself over and over, but couldn't feel it, or any relief, just the itch. Naz's body was hell. It was more than a physical pain, a kind of ongoing heartbreak, almost unbearable.

I stumbled towards a parked car, its side mirror offering another chance at redemption. But there it was again—Naz's face, his eyes wild with my own panic. I reached out to touch the mirror, watching as unfamiliar fingers met their reflection. The disconnect between what I felt and what I saw sent a wave of nausea through me.

"This can't be real," I muttered, but the voice that came out wasn't mine. It was deeper, rougher—Naz's voice escaping from what should have been my throat. I clapped a hand over my mouth, feeling the scratch of a beard that hadn't been there before.

Every movement was a struggle, my brain sending signals to limbs that didn't respond as they should. I tried to walk, but Naz's bow-legged gait made me lurch like a drunken sailor. Each step was a negotiation between my mind and this foreign body.

It took about 25 minutes for me to crawl that heavy body to the front of my building. As I approached, I saw Sean, the security guard I'd known for months, watching me with wary eyes. Hope fluttered in my chest. Surely Sean would recognize me, help me. But as I got closer, I saw him reach for something—a photo.

"I'm supposed to call the police when I see you," he

threatened, holding up a picture of Naz. My heart sank as I realized he was seeing Naz, not me. "I see you're in bad shape, so I'm gonna give you a chance to walk away before I do."

"Please help me," I couldn't feel my tongue very much, but I sent the words the best way I could. "I live here."

Sean's face hardened, a mix of pity and resolve. "Sorry, bro," he persisted, "I can't do anything. One of our residents has given me strict instructions that you cannot be within 100 yards of this building."

I tried to stand straighter, to look Sean in the eye. "Sean, it's me. Walter. From 7D. We talked about the Bulls game just last week, remember?"

Confusion flickered across Sean's face, quickly replaced by suspicion. "I don't know how you know that, but you're not Walter. I know Walter, and you're not him."

"But I am!" I insisted, my voice rising in desperation. "Ask me anything. About the building, about you. Remember when you helped me carry that old TV to the dumpster? Or when I brought you coffee during that night shift last month?"

Sean took a step back, his hand moving to his radio. "Look, I don't know what kind of scam you're trying to pull, but it won't work. Walter's a good kid. You? You're trouble. Now leave before I call the cops."

I could see the fear in Sean's eyes, the way he tensed as if preparing for a fight. And why wouldn't he? In his eyes, I was Naz—a hulking, dangerous-looking man causing a scene. The realization hit me like a punch to the gut. This wasn't just about losing my home; I'd lost every connection, every relationship I'd built.

"Please," I whispered, feeling tears well up in these unfamiliar eyes. "I have nowhere else to go."

For a moment, Sean's resolve seemed to waver. But then he shook his head. "I'm sorry, man. I really am. But you need to leave. Now."

I stood there, rain soaking through my clothes, feeling more lost than ever. This building had been my first real home, the first place I'd felt like I belonged. And now, I was being turned away by someone I'd considered a friend.

What had Naz done to me?

CHAPTER TWELVE

The Caddy was gone, vanished like a mirage. Even if I'd found it, hot-wiring a car wasn't exactly in my skill set. With no other option, I began the long trek to Nona's shop, each step a prayer for respite. Maybe she held the key to unraveling this nightmare, to mending what Naz had broken, or stolen from me. Maybe this was all her idea, to help me in some freakishly odd and messed up way.

Inside Naz's body, an oversized labyrinth of discomfort. My familiar 190-pound frame was now a 320-pound meat-suit. Every move was a challenge. I had to relearn walking. With each step, I felt the weight of his flesh, sludging and sloshing on and off of my spirit. The skin, thick and leathery, like a heavy suit of armor I couldn't remove. The very air seemed to resist my movement, as if the world itself was rejecting this unnatural state.

Expressions were beyond my control, words slurring past my uncooperative lips. When I tried to speak, my voice came out as a gravelly rumble, so unlike my own that it shocked me each time. Loneliness had been my companion for years, but never like this. I was a stranger in new skin, isolated in a way I'd never imagined possible.

"Get away, you fucking drunk!"

There were all kinds of people outside on East 47th Street. Kids hanging out at the corner stores, folks waiting at the bus stop, people selling shit, buying shit, a few others begging. They all disregarded me. Some casting insults, pelting me with rocks as I stumbled along. Even policemen laughed and ignored my cries for help from the comfort of a squad car. Not even my half-dead stroll down the sidewalk would pull their concerns. I couldn't believe it. Told myself it was the smell of stale sweat and street grime that repelled them away.

"Go to Hell, Killer!" were the words of a boy, no more than 14-years-old. Each syllable was a dagger. I'd always been invisible, overlooked, but this... this was active hatred. It was suffocating, crushing. Naz's world was much colder than mine, darker even, like the sky was only gray above him, and it only rained down on his head, no one else's.

Hatred makes the world much harder to bear, and some don't deserve it, no matter what you've seen them have to do.

Each step was a brutal education in hanging on, both mentally and physically. I'd crumble onto the curb, lungs burning, head banging, gasping for breath, but I'd push myself back up, refusing to go out like a punk. Gradually, my spirit started to stretch, trying to fit into this foreign skin. Yet, with every grueling second, a chilling fear gnawed at me: what if I lost myself in this transformation? What if, in becoming Naz, I forgot how to be Walter?

The closer I got to Nona's, the stronger the hate for Naz

grew. Their attacks intensified, sharper objects flying my way, cutting into flesh I hardly felt. I wanted to tell them that I wasn't who I looked like, but that seemed too dangerous to explain at the moment. The pain was distant, muffled, as if my nerves were wrapped in cotton. But the emotional toll... that shit cut deep, raw and immediate.

Then came the gunshots, shattering the air like thunder. A sudden eruption of bullets flying past sent me diving for cover. I hid behind a car, heart pounding as I struggled to make sense of the chaos that unfolded around me.

"I want my intuition, Motherfucker!" a voice bellowed, followed by more shots.

Bullets whizzed over my head, one going straight through the side mirror, inches from the back of my skull. The smell of gunpowder mixed with the stinging stench of fear—my own and that of the panicked bystanders. I risked a peek and saw a man standing in the middle of the street, gun raised, words slurring, not caring about the other people who might witness his terror or get caught in his line of fire. Beside the gunman, a figure loomed, eerily familiar. My body, my face, directing the shooter to aim in my direction.

Naz wore my skin like a new tailored suit, and the sight of it made my stomach churn. He rocked my favorite wheat Timberland boots, army fatigue pants, a White Sox fitted, and a crispy white tee. A long Cuban Link hung from his neck, the same one I'd purchased at Evergreen Plaza. The fool was being me. Every mannerism perfect like he'd known me for years. My slang, the way I stood, and the way that I walked, he had it all down pat. It was like watching a home movie of myself, but one where the actor knew me better than me. Naz's trickery began to make sense. The conversation we had the day before, him repeating my words, copying my walk— the mimicry from yesterday, he was practicing. He studied to become me. Naz had stolen my entire identity. My body, my funds, my car, and my life. I'd fallen for the okey-doke.

I stood up quickly, pointing. "Naz!" I yelled, like I'd sniffed out a burglar and caught him red-handed. "Why'd you do this to me?"

Seeing myself from the outside was surreal, like looking into a mirror that moved independently. A wave of guilt washed over me, my stolen body suddenly feeling alien and wrong in a whole new way.

"There he is!" Naz pointed at me, one hand comfortably resting on the shooter's shoulder, controlling his gun without touching it.

I ran. Broke out towards Nona's, my desperation lending speed to Naz's bulk. Tripped over a vendor's table, knocked their whole display in the mud but couldn't turn back to help due to the chaos behind me. Screams and gunshots. Car alarms and people running for cover in every direction.

"Killer!" The man screamed out. "I'm not fucking around." He fired a few more shots into the air. "I want my intuition." His voice grew distant the farther away I got. The man's shoes were way too nice for him to chase me.

I made my way to Nona's in a panic, my heart pounding in this unfamiliar chest. The chaos of the street faded behind me, replaced by the crash of the welcome bell as I burst through the door. The sudden shift from violence to the peaceful interior of the flower shop was jarring, like stepping from a war zone into a sanctuary.

I ducked behind the window; watched Naz and the gunman cruise by in Slim's Caddy, top down and volume all the way up. Felt like I was straddling two worlds - the dangerous streets I'd just fled and the deceptive calm of Nona's shop. Naz's smile as they passed was pure malice. I'm sure he saw me hiding in the window of his grandmother's shop but he continued pointing forward, guiding the man with the gun to look further ahead. I'd never held my breath for so long, afraid to make a sound as if he could hear me breathing through the walls and the sounds of a crazy Chi-Town street.

Nona came out from her meditation room, saw me, and thought I was Naz. "Boy, I tol' you not to come back here," she scolded, her Creole drawl thick with disapproval. "You bring nothin' but trouble, you."

"I'm shot," I managed to say, suddenly aware of the blood soaking my shirt. The metallic smell of blood mixed with the sweet scent of flowers in the shop, creating a nauseating cocktail.

Nona didn't seem concerned about her grandson's blood leaking all over. She was numb to it. She grabbed a red box from beneath her cash register, pointed to an empty table she likely pruned and repotted a few thousand plants on. "You know de routine."

Grunting and groveling, I made my way to the table, sat on top, and waited for further instruction. The surface was cool against my skin, a stark contrast to the fever heat radiating from my wounds.

"Once I patch you up, I want you to leave out de back door and never return," she said, irritated. "You're very bad vibes for dis place. You're gon' kill all my plants just bein' here."

"Yes, Ma'am," I said respectfully.

"Ma'am?" She asked, suspicious of the sudden display of good manners. Nona straightened her eyeglasses, her eyes locked on mine, and suddenly, she recoiled as if seeing a stranger. She lifted my arm to make sure it was real, then rubbed her eyes and squinted like dust had been thrown in her face. "Who are you, in der?" She asked, creeping closer, eyes of a curious cat. "What de hell is going on?"

I cried like a bitch. An eruption of emotions went through me, like they'd been locked in my dungeon for months.

"Your grandson did this to me! He gave me something, said it was from you, and that it was supposed to fix me," I whined and sobbed.

The story spilled out of me in a rush. Nona's face cycled through disbelief, then anger, and finally, a resigned sadness. "De cologne," she said, "You dat scared little boy from yesterday?"

"Yes! That's me! Walter! Slim's grandson."

Nona squinted her eyes, still staring in mine like she was looking for Naz. Then called off the search.

"What a fine mess you get yourself in, cher." She laughed away her suspicion. "It's hard to surprise ol' Nona, but you got me good with dis."

A police siren screamed past her window, caught our attention. Nona flipped the sign on the door and marked the shop closed for the night. She pulled down the window shade, then locked the doorknob, turned a key to close the top bolt, fastened the latch, and connected a chain.

"You gotta help me," I begged, remembering that the cops might be responding to bullets that were thrown at my face.

"Lie down 'ere, let's see what we can do."

Nona pushed me down on the table, bumped my head right next to a grow light. She ripped my shirt and yanked it from beneath me. A pool of my blood spilled on her floor and she didn't wear a single emotion. Patched me up roughly like a cutman for a fighter who refused to bob and weave.

"I remember this cut," she said while examining the wounds on the skin I was wearing, making sure she tended to them all, old and new. "That boy," she sighed, "hard-headed then, hard-headed now. Always takin', never givin'. Just like your granddaddy. Them all charm an' nothing inside."

"How could I have been so stupid?"

"Yeah, you stupid alright, cher." She chuckled. "But not for dealing with Nazaire. Him a self-absorbed, manipulating, lying piece of shit like all the other men who draw your bloodline. Him fool everyone, no matter how smart. Some people just like dat, ya know. Is a choice, cher. Dey choose dey own hell and bring others down with dem."

"So, what makes you think I'm stupid?"

"Because you don't listen. You emotional first, react second, think last, like all de stupid people in de world tend to do."

Nona poured rubbing alcohol over my wounds, straight from the bottle, no cotton or nothing. I was happy to feel a slight sting, like his skin was beginning to root with whatever it is that I am spiritually made of.

"I tried to warn you about de cologne, it don' just smell good, you know. It cling to your fears, your doubts. Make you weak where you already hurtin'."

"It was too late then, I had already used it for years."

She paused, helped me sit upright. Walked a circle around the table to unroll a long gauze around my midsection, from my waist to my chest.

"Marshalls. You show up strong, smart, charming, tall, and handsome… each one of you. But you nothin' but scared little boys, playin' at bein' a man."

"Damn," was all I could say.

"Wait 'ere, cher."

Nona, that silky old woman, still fit and mad-young in her spirit, switched her hips to the back of her shop, came back minutes later with a dingy white t-shirt and jeans.

"Nazaire is gonna figure you here." She tossed the clothes

on my lap. "I have done all I can to help you, now sneak out de back. You gotta go and see Rune at de boxing gym, over on Racine, across from Leon's BBQ. He's sure to know how to help you."

"Rune?" I asked, my voice catching in my throat, hoping I had heard the name wrong. The very mention of it sent a chill down my spine. Rune was more than just a man; he was a living legend, co-founder of one of the most notorious street gangs in Chicago. His reputation was built on violence and fear, a name whispered in dark alleys and avoided in daylight conversations. They said he once knocked a man's head clean off his neck with a single uppercut—an act that had become myth, but no less terrifying for it. The thought of crossing paths with him made my blood run cold.

Nona sighed, lowering her head. "No need to worry, cher. Rune's a good man now," she said, her voice gentle but sure. "No more of that gangster stuff. He's turned his life around, dedicatin' himself to keepin' kids outta the gangs. You see him on TV every summer, marchin' with Rev. Toney, standin' up for the community. He gives free haircuts, teaches the boys how to box. He's helpin' boys your age like they're his own, tryin' to give 'em the chances he never had."

"I know where to go, I used to hide in the field house at Moran Park, just down the street from his gym."

"Go dere now, but I warn you, he won't be very happy to see you."

I put my head down, asked, "What other choice do I have?" moving low and discouraged.

Nona placed her hand on my shoulder, the glint of those hidden blades in her rings catching my eye. She tried to calm me with her touch, but the sharp, dangerous edges of those blades were a stark reminder that I could very well still be in danger. Even in this moment of reassurance, I couldn't quite shake the unease those rings brought.

"My grandson... He been through so much. He know no other way. Please have mercy wid him."

"How can I beat him? He's slick, he's a liar, and he has full control of my life."

Nona nodded, but her eyes were sad. "De only way I know how to beat any man is by attacking his pride. You cripple him dat way, den you both the same size for a fair and even fight. It's what nature would want."

CHAPTER THIRTEEN

It was a long walk from East 47th Street to 59th and Racine, but the practice I needed to operate my arrangement at a higher degree. Every pothole a trap, every shadow a potential ambush. My new body felt like a beacon, drawing hostile gazes from every corner. How many more of these people, I wondered, had fallen victim to Naz's cruel games?

The gym loomed ahead, a weathered sanctuary of sweat and redemption. The faded sign barely clung to life; you could hardly make out the name of the place. However, a logo of a black Popeye the Sailor-looking character, wearing a determined grin and red boxing gloves, still cut through the grime.

A commotion erupted behind me. A woman's voice, raw

with fury, cut through the air as she burst out of Leon's BBQ. Her eyes locked on me as she charged in my direction. "Nazaire... Marshall... Lacoste..." she called out, her words echoing with an intensity that turned heads.

I turned to face a woman who looked like she had spent years weathering life's storms. A black and white bonnet clung to her head, and she shuffled in flip-flops, a camisole slipping from her shoulders. Dark, worried circles around her eyes.

Despite the weariness etched into her features, there was an undeniable beauty to her—a face untouched by time, a body that defied the hardships she'd endured. But in her eyes, I saw a graveyard of broken promises, and I knew instantly that her pain would soon be mine to bear.

"I HATE YOU! You worthless bastard!" she screamed, yanking off her shoes and flinging them at me with a fury that felt personal.

I raised my hands, trying to defuse her rage. "Hey, calm down! Let's talk about this!"

But she was far beyond talking. "I HATE YOU! I HATE YOU!" she kept shouting, her voice cracking with years of pent-up anger.

I didn't have the words to soothe her. I didn't know the history, the pain she carried because of Naz. All I could do was offer an apology for the hurt I wasn't even sure of.

"I'm sorry," I said, my voice soft, trying to convey a guilt I didn't fully understand.

Her eyes widened, a bitter smile twisting her lips as if my words were salt on an open wound. "Sorry? That's all you've got?"

She let her shoes drop to the floor and plunged at me, her nails digging into my forearm with a ferocity that should have sent shockwaves of pain through my body. But instead of agony, all I felt was a dull pressure, a reminder of how far gone I was from feeling anything real. I realized this was what he meant by being disconnected—numb to the physical, but not to the guilt that gnawed at the edges of my consciousness.

Another woman, around the same age as the one in the black and white bonnet, stormed out of Leon's and grabbed the girl, pulling her back with a mixture of frustration and concern. "Come on, Crystal," she said, rolling her eyes and neck. "He's not even worth it."

Crystal resisted at first, but then broke free for one last, venomous strike. She jabbed her finger at the center of my forehead, her voice low and cutting. "You used to be somebody, Killer. Now you're just a joke of a father who can't even be bothered to visit his own son."

I could have defended myself, could have told her the truth she didn't know. But I let her words sink in, allowed her to punish me, to relieve the anger she carried. She needed an outlet, and maybe I deserved it. Maybe I needed to feel the weight of those words, even if they weren't meant for me. I mumbled another apology, hollow and inadequate, knowing it wouldn't change a thing.

Her friend finally managed to pull her away, dragging her

across Racine Street. But Crystal's gaze lingered, filled with disappointment and hurt that stung deeper than her punches or scratches. I turned away, allowed the shame to wash over me.

I had traded my rock-bottom for his—a man years older, with a lifetime of missteps and people he'd taken for granted. I found myself walking in the shoes of someone who had betrayed not just his family, but the entire city of Chicago. A man who lied about his own grandmother, who stole from kids, who killed without remorse, and who couldn't even bring himself to visit his own son. What kind of monster was Naz? The more I thought about it, the more I felt a deep, festering hatred for myself.

As I stepped into the gym, the air hit me like a wall, thick with the stench of stale sweat and worn leather. The place was guarded by a crew of broken-nosed brawlers, their faces etched with scars that mapped out a lifetime of hard-won battles. There wasn't a single smile among them—only the silent promise of violence simmering just beneath the surface.

They circled me, a pack of wolves sizing up wounded prey. I could feel their hunger, their desire to tear into the man they thought I was. "I didn't come here to fight," I said, the words sounding hollow even to my own ears. "I just want to talk to Rune."

The standoff stretched, tension coiling tighter with each passing second. I looked around, found an office sign above a door in the back, started easing towards that.

"Dead man walking." One man called out, patting his fist in his palm to warm it up for my face.

"Stupid motherfucker came back," another man said.

Then, like a thunderclap, the office door open and slammed. The fighters parted, revealing a figure that commanded respect with his mere presence.

He moved with a fluid grace that belied his age, each step purposeful and measured. Muscles rippled beneath skin adorned with a tapestry of tattoos, telling stories I could only imagine. His scalp gleamed in the dim light, and behind thick-rimmed glasses, his eyes held a wisdom that seemed to pierce beyond me.

This had to be Rune.

He slipped through the nearest ropes with the ease of a man half his age, bouncing on the balls of his feet. "Come on," he said, his voice a raspy purr. "A little spar for old time's sake."

It wasn't a request.

I weighed my options, eyeing the exit. But Rune's crew stood ready, knuckles cracking ominously. With a resigned sigh, I climbed into the ring.

A kid, no more than ten, approached to tape my hands. His fingers trembled, eyes wide with fear.

As I knelt to lace up my gloves, I closed my eyes and whispered a prayer. Not for victory, but for understanding. For a way out of this nightmare.

The fight began without ceremony, just the bloodthirsty

cheers of Rune's crew. "KICK HIS ASS, RUNE!"

Rune's eyes never left mine as he circled, smashed his fists together like the Hulk. "Let's see if you still got it, big man."

I raised my gloves, mouth dry. "Look, I didn't come here to —"

His fist interrupted my plea, a lightning-fast jab that should have sent pain exploding through my jaw. Instead, I just felt the impact, the way my hands feel after hammering wood. Before I could process it, two hooks slammed into my gut, followed by an uppercut that lifted me off my feet.

I crashed to the canvas, the gym spinning in five directions around me. Rune loomed overhead, disgust etched on his face. "I'm not falling for your lies anymore." His foot connected with my ribs, a sickening crack echoing through the gym, blood soaked through my bandages.

Still, very little physical pain. Just... pressure. As I spat blood onto the canvas, a strange calm settled over me. I couldn't have much pain, so what the hell was I scared of?

I pushed myself up, newfound determination straightening my spine. Rune's eyebrow quirked, a flicker of surprise crossing his face. "First time I ever saw you get knocked down," he mused. "Next time you ain't getting back up."

"I'm not who you think I am," I said, the words coming out stronger than I expected.

Rune's laugh was sharp. "Oh yeah? Prove it."

I swung, wild and clumsy in this borrowed body. Rune danced away, his movements fluid and precise. "What the hell was that?" he taunted. "Hit me like you mean it!"

Frustration bubbled up inside me. I lunged again, throwing haymakers that wouldn't have hit the broad side of a barn. Rune weaved and bobbed, landing stinging jabs that I knew should have hurt.

"You've got power," he said, circling me like a shark, "but power means nothing if you can't land a punch."

I stumbled, crashing to the canvas again. The gym erupted

in laughter, the sound grating against my ears.

Rune's voice cut through the noise. "I know I taught you better than that. Come on, use your head. Fighting isn't just about strength. You know that!"

Rune danced around the ring, shuffling his feet like Ali in celebration. He moved around from one spot to the next, nonstop, keeping his focus on me.

I pushed myself up once more, planting my feet with purpose. Sweat stung my eyes, but I blinked it away, zeroing in on Rune. Looked beyond the tattoos and the muscles, his quick feet and hands. I saw the intelligence in his eyes, the way he read every micro-movement of my body. I had to be smart in my attack, wait for him to dance his way back onto my path.

"I'm not Naz," I said, the words ringing with truth.

"Not Naz?" Rune was in shock, paralyzed by a certain awareness. "What?"

He let his guard down suddenly, in mid fight, a big no no. I was already swinging, wildly threw a jab through the first opening, my fist connecting with his jaw. He flew backwards, crashing into the ropes before slumping to the canvas.

The gym fell silent, a collective intake of breath as everyone processed what they'd just witnessed. Rune lay still for a moment, then... he laughed, came up on one knee. A deep, genuine belly laugh that seemed to shake the very foundations of the building.

He propped himself up on one elbow, rubbing his jaw. "Well, I'll be damned," he chuckled. "Not bad, kid. Not bad at all for a first-timer."

I offered him a hand, pulling him up to his feet. He studied me, really studied me, like he was seeing me for the first time. Then he looked around the room, noticed how impatient his goons were, locked on high alert, ready to pounce and have his back.

He whispered to me, "Who are you?"

"How did you know?" I countered, relief washing over my

soul.

Rune's smile was enigmatic. "Eyes don't lie, son. And those ain't Killer's eyes looking out at me." He waved off his crew. "Alright, everybody out. I should have a private chat with my son."

Rune reached out a hand, and I reluctantly helped him through the ropes while the gym cleared out, only one man remaining, refusing to trust me with Rune.

"Your son?" I asked.

"Practically. I sure treated him like one, pro'bly more than my own. Had a fall out with my actual family because of it, and Naz still fucked me over in the end."

We talked all the way to the office in back, settled into a battered leather chair, myself on the opposite couch, then talked some more. The office was a chaotic jumble of used boxing equipment scattered haphazardly. A dozen empty water bottles littered the floor, mingling with VHS tapes stacked precariously against the wall, each label marked with nothing more than the year, month, and day. An open first aid kit spilled its contents across a dusty desk, bandages and antiseptic wipes strewn about. The blinds on the window were broken down, offering no privacy, their slats hanging like the ribs of a dilapidated skeleton. And it stunk in there too, a foul mix of sweat, old leather, and garbage can with no lid. It was an assault on the senses, much like the revelations I'd been facing. Yet, there was also a sense of authenticity to it all, a raw honesty that matched Rune's no-nonsense reputation.

"So," he said, leaning back in his chair, "tell me how you ended up jiving with Naz."

"I drank a strange liquid he gave me, thought it was from Nona. I foolishly believed he was trying to help me."

"You're not a fool seeking help for problems, but what made you think a man called Killer Naz would be a solution?"

"How'd he do it to you?" I blurted out, my words driven purely by emotion. "He fucked you over the same way, didn't he?" I couldn't help but channel all my feelings of stupidity and hurl them back to the source from which they came.

Rune dismissed my projection with a sneer, leaned forward, and locked his gaze on me, as if searching for me within the confines of my large, imposing figure. His hands were planted on his desk, fists clenched tightly. "You want to rephrase that?" he asked, his voice dripping with menace. Rune was still very much a gangster, and he loathed having to remind me of that fact.

I took a deep gulp, ingested my saliva and my pride in one swallow. "He's my cousin." I said. A much better response.

Rune sat back in his chair. Popped a toothpick in his mouth and began chewing on it. It seemed to put him at ease.

"Cousin? That boy don't give a damn about family," Rune laughed. "His daddy's been in jail all his life, momma overdosed on some drugs. Nona's the only person who actually gave him a chance, but I have proof she used to touch on that boy." Rune sucked his teeth and played with the toothpick in his mouth. "Family,'" he said with a smirk. "Killer don't know what it feels like."

"Well, I thought family was supposed to be tight and be there for each other."

"You're talking about a good family. Most families. But not all families are like that. Be happy Naz ain't your family, kid. You don't even know him."

"But, I'm Cadillac Slim's grandson," I stammered, my hands shaking. "Nona said that Slim is Naz's grandfather."

Rune's demeanor shifted, his expression growing more serious. He leaned forward again, this time with a look of genuine concern etched across his face. "You said you're Slim's grandson?" he asked, his voice then carried a burden.

"Yes! My name is Walter. I'm Sage's son, maybe Melvin's. Who knows?"

"Damn," Rune finally said, shaking his head. "I always knew that cologne was trouble." Slim thought he was so slick, but he never understood the price of power."

"You knew Slim?" I asked, leaning forward.

Rune's laugh was tinged with sadness. "Knew him? Slim was my dawg before he started dealing with the sweaty cologne."

Back down memory lane. This time with Rune, telling me more about Slim—things that Sergeant Wilson didn't know.

"We were enemies once," he continued, "before a mutual endeavor. After that, everything between us became a friendly competition. Who could get the most girls, who could drive the best car and flyest suits. As if that wasn't bad enough, Slim felt the need to take it further. He got drunk off the praises he got from the people he knew. Attention was his addiction—chasing their approval no matter the cost. He always needed someone to tell him how great he was for this, and how smooth he was for that. Any compliment would do. When those compliments ran low, he felt he needed something outside of himself to get it done. That's when that smelly cologne came into play. Someone dropped it off at his door on his birthday, more than 50 years ago, and it never runs out.

I saw how it changed him, how it changed everybody around him. I did the smart thing and left him alone. Slim would call and I would place him on hold. Slim would come and I would go the other way. I had things going on of my own, and I didn't want to make my life worse or get caught in his mess."

He stood, pacing the small office. "That cologne? It's a crutch. A shortcut. And shortcuts always come with a cost."

I absorbed his words, feeling like I was finally getting some answers. "So how do I fix this? How do I get my body back?"

Rune stopped pacing and fixed me with a penetrating gaze. "You're asking the wrong question, kid. You say you want your body back, but that's not what you should be chasing. What you need to focus on is your life."

He paused, letting his words sink in before continuing. "Killer doesn't have your life; he's got things that once belonged to you—a suit, maybe a few trinkets. What you're really after isn't just the physical stuff; it's the essence of who you are and what you were meant to be. Chasing after your body is like trying to reclaim a shadow. What you need to do is reclaim your life—the dreams, the purpose, the people who matter."

Rune leaned in closer, his voice dropping to a more intense tone. "It's about more than just getting back what was taken. It's about finding what makes you whole, and knowing what gives your life meaning so you'll never think you've lost it again."

His words hit me like a punch to the gut—one that I could actually feel. "But... how?" I asked, my voice small.

"That's the journey, kid. It starts with understanding who you are, beyond the skin you're in." He leaned in, his voice low and intense. "You threw that punch earlier not because you're in Naz's body, but because there's something trapped inside this colossal body worth fighting for. That's where your power comes from. Not some magic cologne, not someone else's muscles. No one else can tell you what you are. The answer has to come out of you."

CHAPTER FOURTEEN

Nona didn't have any answers; she sent me to Rune. Rune had no answers either; he sent me back to myself. I thought he was just being philosophical—something I didn't have the luxury of. I had worked hard with that body: all those sit-ups and push-ups, the haircuts, the growing up. My hands had saved me from falling, had touched the most beautiful things. My eyes had seen the stunning lakefront, the architecture of Chicago, and its unique skyline. My ears have heard Miles Davis, Coltrane, the voice of Sade, and beats brought to life by Dilla and the RZA. My feet, my legs, my chest, my torso— we shared countless special memories. It'd be foolish to let them all go without a fight.

No other motion but to fight for myself. I took a night's

rest in the back of Rune's gym, and got up early the next morning, 6 a.m., when the most dedicated boxers came in to stretch out and warm up their gloves. I left them there to do work, took a nice long jog to Hyde Park.

Slipped through the alley behind my building, careful to stay in the shadows. Scaling the fire escape, each rung and ledge felt familiar under my fingers. Reaching the seventh floor, I pried open the window I knew was always loose and climbed into my condo.

I landed silently in the dimly lit living room, my eyes adjusting to the darkness. The air was thick with the scent of unfamiliar cologne, bad-smelling incense, and the lingering aroma of takeout food. My stomach churned at the intrusion of foreign smells in my space.

The first thing I noticed was the orderliness. The last time I'd been here, the place was a mess—papers and clothes thrown everywhere, dishes piled high in the sink. Now, everything was neat and clean, almost sterile. The transformation was jarring, like walking into a stranger's home wearing my skin.

Moving cautiously, I scanned every detail. I opened my closets and found them filled with clothes I would never wear —flashy-colored jogging pants, oversized t-shirts with brand names printed on the front like billboards, loud-colored jackets, and expensive gym shoes. My tailor-made suits and designer clothes were gone, replaced with these cheap, tasteless outfits.

As I rifled through drawers and cabinets, I stumbled upon a leather-bound journal hidden beneath a stack of papers. I flipped it open, and my blood ran cold.

Page after page was filled with obsessive ramblings about Hope. Detailed accounts of her daily routines, her likes and dislikes, even sketches of her face. It was then that the horrifying truth hit me: Naz wasn't just some random cousin who'd stolen my identity. He was Hope's ex-boyfriend, the one she'd told me about, the one who haunted her nightmares.

"That evil motherfucker!"

My hands shook with fury as I continued to read. Naz hadn't taken my body for the money or the cologne. He'd done it all for Hope. To get close to her again, to manipulate her in the cruelest way possible.

I slammed the journal shut, my breath coming in ragged gasps as I struggled to contain my rage. This wasn't just about me anymore. Naz had made it personal in a way I couldn't have imagined. He'd violated not just my life, but Hope's trust, her sense of safety, her very reality.

Determined, ready to confront Killer, I decided to wait. I armed myself with a heavy flashlight, its cold metal a comforting weight in my hand. I crouched in the darkest corner of the living room, my heart pounding hard as I prepared to confront the man who had stolen my life. Hours passed, each minute stretching into eternity. The tick of the clock on the wall seemed to grow louder with each passing second, a constant reminder of the time slipping away.

Then, I heard the sound of keys jangling outside the front door. My muscles tensed, ready to spring, and my grip tightened on the flashlight. My breath got caught in my throat when the door creaked open. It wasn't Naz who walked in—it was Hope.

She stumbled slightly, her movements unsteady. The sharp scent of alcohol wafted into the room as she crossed her feet and walked in a zigzag to flop on the couch. The sight of her, vulnerable and out of place.

I stepped out from the shadows, my heart pounding with a mix of shock and dread. Hope saw me and froze, her eyes wide with fear and disbelief. I never expected her to come here, especially not now. She had no idea she was in danger, and seeing her there filled me with a rising sense of panic.

"You!" she screamed, her voice slicing through the silence as she backed toward the door. Her hand dove into her purse, and for a moment, I braced for a weapon. Instead, she pulled out a panic button, pressing it repeatedly. Along with it came a crumpled piece of paper, worn from too many readings. "This court order says you're not supposed to be within 100 yards of me!"

I raised my hands in surrender.

"Hope, it's not what you think—"

"I know exactly what it is!" she shouted, her voice trembling with emotion. "You're a monster, Naz!"

I took a deep breath, my mind racing. "Hope, please listen to me. I'm not Naz. It's a long story, but you have to believe me."

Her eyes flickered with confusion and anger. For a split second, I saw a hint of doubt cross her face, as if something in my words or tone had struck a chord. But it quickly vanished, replaced by renewed fury. "What kind of sick game are you playing this time?"

I took a step closer, my voice urgent but gentle. "The man you're with is a—"

"Get away from me!" she screamed, grabbing anything

within reach—a lamp, a vase—and hurling them at me. The crash of breaking glass filled the air. "I don't want to hear your lies!"

"Hope, please!" I dodged the flying objects, desperation creeping into my voice. The scent of her perfume, mixed with alcohol, filled my nostrils as I moved closer, grabbed her by the shoulders to prevent her from swinging. "Look at me! Look in my eyes!"

Hope screamed at the top of her lungs. Put the whole building on alert. I put her down in a hurry and took a step back.

"I didn't mean to—"

"Stay away from me!" she shrieked. Grabbed a chair and swung it at me. A whoosh of air hit my face as it missed me by inches.

I tried to approach her again, my heart breaking at her fear and fury. "Hope, you have to believe me. I found his journal. He's obsessed with you. He wrote about you, how he's been stalking you for years. He's dangerous!"

She paused for a split second, her breath coming in ragged gasps. Hope shook her head violently, as if trying to clear it, and renewed her assault. "You're lying! You're always lying! The only danger around here is from you."

That's around when the sound of approaching sirens filled the air, their wailing growing louder by the second. My heart sank as I realized time was running out. I turned to face the door, ready to face whatever came next. The police car screeched to a halt outside, and officers poured out, guns drawn.

"Look, I have his journal right here." I pat the sides of my pocket and searched for the journal that was no longer there. Scanned around the condo, saw it across the room on the floor, where I'd hidden in the corner to surprise Killer Naz.

I took one step forward and the door burst open with a thunderous crash. Several officers rushed in, shouting commands. "Hands up! On the ground!"

I raised my hands, my mind racing. Went down on my knees and allowed the police officers to fasten the cuffs. I looked over at Hope, who talked to the officers hysterically. Heard her say she thought she was going to die. I looked over towards the corner where the journal lied flat on the floor.

"Hope, there's the journal by the door. Read it. It'll tell you everything you need to know." I sang. I turned to the officer who cuffed me, still down on my knees, said, "Read it. You'll see."

"You mean this book here?" Naz said as he entered the room, wearing my most expensive suit, groomed to perfection, even had a beard shading in that I'd been trying to grow.

Naz picked up the book, went right to the back page and showed it to the officer. "Says here, property of Nazaire Marshall Lacoste." Then looked at me and smiled. "Hey, man. You've got a cool name. Is that Creole?"

I jumped up, swung my shoulder at Naz with my hands still

cuffed behind my back. Missed him by inches but crashed through the wall and into the hallway, plaster dust filling the air.

"Stop him!" one of the officers yelled. I wasn't planning to run, but my adrenaline kicked up. Shoved the officers aside and burst through the back stairs. I was far too desperate to hold.

When I hit the street, I barely glanced back. The cool night air slapped my face as I sprinted away, hands still cuffed behind my back. All I could think about was survival, about finding a way to rescue Hope from the nightmare of Naz.

CHAPTER FIFTEEN

I saw Sage today; shuffling down the hallway of our shared prison. He looked pitiful, eyes fixed on the floor, probably only recognizing people by their shoes and legs now.

One nurse told me he hadn't eaten a full meal in months, and you could see it in his weight loss. When I first came to see him in this place, before I was confined to it myself, Sage was large and powerful, arms like Mike Tyson's. Now he's frail and malnourished, walking around with worry in his eyes. I try to talk to him sometimes, but it seems he can only return a blank stare. Nothing is there.

Here I am, locked up in the same institution as the man who just might be my father. We're from different worlds, different times, and yet we've ended up in the same damned place. It's like the universe has a sick sense of humor, bringing us together in this sterile, hopeless environment.

As I watch him disappear around the corner, I can't help but wonder: is this my future, too? Will I become just another shuffling, broken Marshall man? The thought gives me chills, making me think of what happened on that old rooftop and wonder what I could've done differently to not wind up in this place...

The rooftop I speak of was my old sanctuary, my vantage point into a life that was no longer mine. It sat atop an old brick building directly across the alley from my former apartment. The positioning couldn't have been more perfect if I'd designed it myself. From there, I had an unobstructed view into the living room and bedroom windows of what used to be my home.

I'd discovered it by chance, really. Desperate for a way to keep an eye on Hope without being seen, I scoured the neighborhood until I found this hidden gem. The building itself was empty, scheduled for renovation but caught in some bureaucratic bullshit. For me, it was a Godsend. I fashioned a makeshift bunker from old tarps and debris, creating a hidden nook where I could observe undetected. I'd even rigged up a crude periscope using mirrors and PVC pipe, allowing me to survey the street below without exposing myself.

This rooftop wasn't just a place to watch; it became my command center, my home base for an operation I never thought I'd be running. There, I plotted, planned, and prayed. There, I watched the life I once had play out before me like some twisted theater production.

And it was from that perch that I began my vigil, my desperate attempt to reclaim what was stolen from me...

Day 1: The concrete of the rooftop bit into my palms as I lay prone, makeshift binoculars pressed to my eyes. The city was alive, a maze of lights and shadows, but my focus was singular: the window of my old apartment. I felt a twinge of guilt. Was this really necessary? But as I caught a glimpse of

Hope through the glass, I steeled my resolve. I had to protect her, no matter the cost.

Day 5: I'd become a shadow, trailing Hope through the city. Today, I followed her from her art class to the grocery store, then to the park. I ducked behind bushes, ignoring the thorns that tore at my skin. At one point, I nearly twisted my ankle leaping behind a dumpster when she unexpectedly turned around. The physical pain is nothing compared to the ache in my chest every time I see her smile at a stranger, unaware of the danger she's in. I know this behavior is bordering on obsessive, but what choice do I have? I'm the only one who knows the truth.

Day 9: The rooftop had become my second home, the city my unwitting ally. Today, my focus shifted from Hope to the police car parked outside my building. I meticulously noted their patterns—Officer Johnson's cigarette breaks at 10 AM and 2 PM, Officer Rodriguez's habit of circling the block on foot every three hours. Their routines became a map in my mind, each detail a potential opening. I jotted down notes; a plan began to form.

Day 12: Naz's words echoed in my mind: "Nona can make a tea that makes liars tell the truth." The solution seemed so simple. Get the tea from Nona, somehow make Naz drink it in Hope's presence, and watch his lies unravel. With renewed purpose, I made my way to Nona's shop, hope blooming in my chest for the first time in days.

The scene that greeted me shattered that hope like glass. It was after hours and the doors of the shop had been left wide open. I was suspicious immediately when I crept inside. In the backroom, Nona sat in a chair, rocking back and forth, mumbling incoherently. Drool trickled from her bone-dry lips, hair all over her head, bloodshot eyes staring vacantly at a TV that wasn't even tuned on a proper channel. A blanket was wrapped around her, her feet soaking in a basin of water that had long gone cold.

The smell of decay hit me as I approached. Flies buzzed

around where she sat. Next to Nona, a microwave TV dinner sat untouched, days old by the look of it. My stomach churned as I noticed a piece of paper tucked under the tray. With trembling hands, I unfolded the note:

"Anyone who helps you is dead to me."

The words were clearly left for me to find. Naz had been there. He'd done that to Nona, reduced that vibrant woman to a shell, all to send me a message. The full weight of what I was up against crashed down on me. Naz was dangerous and getting more fucked up by the minute, more than I'd ever imagined. And he was always one step ahead.

I knelt beside Nona, gently taking her hand. "I'm so sorry," I whispered, though I knew she couldn't hear me. "I'll make this right. I promise."

Panic surged through me as I realized Rune could be next. Without a second thought, I bolted out of the shop and started running towards his gym. As I ran, I marveled at the strength and endurance of Naz's body. I wasn't even winded, my powerful legs eating up the distance effortlessly. It was fitting more and more by the moment, and I wasn't really sure how to take it all in.

As I rounded the corner to Rune's gym, my heart sank. An ambulance and five cop cars were parked outside, lights flashing silently. Paramedics were wheeling someone out on a stretcher, a white sheet covering the body. Rune's goons stood nearby, their faces a mix of anger and grief. Some were openly weeping.

I skidded to a stop, my mind reeling. Was that Rune under that sheet?

"Fuck! I'm too late."

I had a mini tantrum, swinging my fists through the air, wildly aiming at nothing. I wanted to rush forward, to demand answers, but the place was crawling with cops. I couldn't risk it.

Naz was systematically destroying everyone who could help me, isolating me, cutting off all my options. That rooftop was the only place I could go, the only place I felt safe. No one occupied that building; a few crackheads broke in every once in a while, but there was nothing to take, nothing for me to defend. I found solace in knowing that no one would be hurt because of me. Most nights, I stayed there, staring at the stars, watching the streetlights flicker until I fell asleep.

This place pulls me back to that rooftop, to those nights when I was lost in the cracks of the city, trying to find myself in the wrong places. The way these fluorescent lights buzz and flicker in the sterile hallways of the University of Chicago Hospital for Mental Health—they're just as unforgiving as the concrete I used to sit on, palms pressed against the cold, rough surface. I can still feel that grit digging into my skin, like it was trying to anchor me in that abandoned building, a forgotten space where the air was thick with must and despair.

CHAPTER SIXTEEN

Watching Naz and Hope frolic around my crib like a happy couple from that rooftop had become a daily routine. I didn't know what else to do. I pretended to act as the savior she once believed me to be—some kind of whacked-out guardian angel.

The city was active as usual, its veins pulsing with a thousand stories, each one tangled in a web of light and shadow. The kind of place where secrets thrived and people did God-knows-what to survive. The air had turned cool, that Lake Michigan breeze cutting through the streets like a blade, reminding you how fragile comfort could be when the roof over your head was more theory than fact. Chicago had a way of wrapping itself around you like autumn—chilly, sometimes cold, always beautiful. The weather, the people—both as unpredictable as the city itself, but that's what made it all so damn irresistible.

One evening, as the sun dipped below the horizon, casting long shadows across the city, I saw them. Hope and Naz, in the living room. Through my makeshift binoculars, I watched as Naz reached for something at my bar. My breath caught in my throat as I recognized the familiar blue bottle of the Sweaty Cologne sitting right on the counter, joined by that funky vial of whatever, sitting right in its shadow.

Naz sprayed the cologne on himself, the mist catching the last rays of sunlight. Then he danced around the corner like a simp, making Hope laugh as he invited her to join in the groove. They danced for a minute, pissing me off when they started kissing. That motherfucker rubbed his stolen hands around her body, squeezing and grabbing her ass like a melon, grinding on her midsection like a young Patrick Swayze. My heart shattered into a million pieces, blood boiling. She had no idea of the deception, of the violation.

The two of them wouldn't stop kissing. I had flashbacks of our night in the park—the way her breath eased from those lips when she moaned, the way she swirled and ground her body on me, the way she bit my chest and dug her nails in my back when I was on her. Naz was likely getting it like that. I couldn't bear to watch them touch anymore. I had to do something—anything.

I grabbed a brick from the rooftop, its rough surface cool against my palm. With a grunt of frustration, I hurled it through the window. The glass shattered with a satisfying crash, the sound echoing off the surrounding buildings. I ducked behind the ledge, my heart pounding with excitement. Naz ran to the window with a gun, cursing at the people on the street below, but he didn't see me. The cop outside glanced up but couldn't figure out where the brick had come from.

I stayed hidden, watching Naz's reaction. He slammed the broken window shut, more glass falling to the floor, and continued cursing, his frustration evident. Hope looked scared and confused when she answered the door and talked to the policemen investigating the incident. I stayed low, laughing inside while watching it all through a peephole I made, just big enough to slide my fake binoculars through.

Naz came out the back with their jackets, keys in hand, walking out the door with Hope and the cops. I saw the vial and the cologne still sitting on the counter. I saw an opportunity, so I jumped up and ran downstairs.

The stairwell echoed with my footsteps as I descended, the smell of mildew and old cigarettes growing stronger with each floor. My heart raced, pumping adrenaline through my veins. As I burst out of the building's back door, the cool night air hit me like a slap to the face.

The wide alley, just big enough for a garbage truck to slide through, dumpsters lining one side, their pungent odor mixing with the city's usual bouquet of exhaust fumes and greasy food from nearby restaurants. Graffiti adorned the brick walls, vibrant colors stark against the dingy backdrop. In the distance, sirens wailed—the urban lullaby.

Leaning against the rough brick wall, I felt confidence building inside me. I remembered the raw power I had felt when I broke away from the police and smashed through a wall. I was stronger now, more capable than I had ever been in my old body. I was finally ready to use that strength to get my life back.

I peered around the corner, watching the building. Hope and Naz stepped out, heading toward the Caddy. My heart twisted, seeing Hope's sad face. She looked uncomfortable, a shadow of the happiness she used to radiate. It was clear she didn't really want to go wherever Naz was taking her.

I was set to storm the place, thinking raw force could get me in and out with that damn cologne and vial. No plan on what to do with it, but if it was Naz's ace, I'd take it just to twist the knife. My newfound strength? I could've made the same getaway as before. I was seconds from charging in when cold steel pressed against the back of my skull, stopping me dead in my tracks.

"Where's my intuition, you Mr. T-looking motherfucker?"

I sighed, already tired of being threatened. I figured my only chance would be to outsmart him, which should be easy to do with a man who claims to have lost his sense of foresight and insight.

"Listen, bro." With my finger, I pointed up toward the bedroom window of my old apartment.

"I ain't yo bro. I'm Osiris." He cocked the gun.

"Well, Osiris," I continued, "the guy who lives in that apartment got away with all the magic. I'm trying to get in there and get it back so I can undo all the nasty shit I've done, but there's a cop around the corner, waiting to arrest me the moment he sees me."

Osiris pressed the barrel harder against my skull, then leaned across me to see Officer Rodriguez staking out around the corner. "How do I know you're not lying?"

I turned slowly, looked the man in his eyes with my hands up to show I wasn't a threat. "Look at me, I'm a large worthless piece of shit with no home, no food, and nothing or nobody to give a damn about. I've lost everything because of all the nasty shit I've done. Tired of living like this." I pouted. Thought about pursuing a career in acting after all this is over.

Osiris slapped both sides of my face with the front and back of his left hand. He pointed up to the window of my old apartment and asked, "All the magic shit is up there?"

"Yup."

Osiris raised the gun away from my face, using it to scratch the top of his head, as if it helped him think more clearly. I had him on the fence.

"You don't have to worry." I added a little reassurance. "That's the lack of intuition in your brain, making you doubt yourself. But what's your reputation? You were a precise, confident man before I came around. You were a boss. A decision-maker who didn't question things that made sense.

Now look at you, about to shoot the only person alive who can help you."

Osiris slapped me again. It gave him a false sense of control, so I allowed it. Then he said, "I wouldn't be in this shit if it wasn't for you." And although he had believed I was Naz, I somehow felt I deserved it.

"I have a plan," I continued, slowly lowering his gun with my hand. "If you want any chance of getting your intuition back, you need to help me. We need to get inside that condo and get the vial of liquid magic and magic cologne spray."

He hesitated, the gun wavering. A few more seconds of heavy thinking, then he turned to me with the eye of the tiger and asked, "Where are they?"

I gave him detailed instructions. "The cologne and vial are both sitting on a counter, near the bar area. Just get in, grab them, and get out. I'll be here, waiting."

He looked at me for a long moment, then nodded. "Fine. But if you're lying..."

"I'm not," I assured him. "Just hurry; I don't know how much longer the place will be empty."

Osiris straightened his clothing, a sharp all-white Nautica short-set that was made for the fall season, matching white Nautica shoes, cap, expensive sunglasses, and watch. I watched him walk inside the building like he owned the place, pretending to talk on his flip phone. He shook a cop's hand and asked directions to the elevator, with the gun bulging out from the back of his shirt. The cops didn't notice—too busy looking for me.

I watched the light in the apartment go on, totally unadvised. Minutes felt like hours, then the lights went back off. Then I saw him coming out, walking suspiciously past the policemen with a small bottle clutched in one hand, the other hand inside his jacket.

Homie walked out of the building with his eyes darting around nervously. His steps were quick and cautious, and for a moment, it seemed he would make it to me without incident.

His face was pale, though—a sheen of sweat visible even in the dim light of the street lamps. I should've known right then what was up.

As he neared, our eyes locked for a brief moment. Relief started to wash over me, but then something in Osiris's expression changed. Panic flickered across his face, his grip tightening on the stolen items. Without warning, he spun on his heel and bolted in the opposite direction.

"Osiris, wait!" I shouted, but my words were lost in the cold Chicago wind. Desperation kicked in, and I began to chase after him, my footsteps echoing off the buildings as I closed in on the distance between us.

Osiris ran with frantic energy, glancing over his shoulder only once before putting on another burst of speed. My breath came in gasps, the chill air burning my lungs. Just as I was gaining ground, he turned his head slightly and fired two shots behind him without breaking his stride.

The bullets whizzed past, one of them embedding itself in

the brick wall beside me. I had to stop chasing, my heart pounding in my chest. I watched helplessly as Osiris disappeared into the night, his silhouette swallowed by the darkness. He clung to the vial and cologne and ran like Devin Hester, leaving me with nothing but the gnawing sense that time was running out.

November 15, 2002

To the woman who believes what she sees in her dreams,

I pray that this letter has not disturbed you, and I will do my very best to ensure that the message within is delivered as gently as my pen can write.

Hope,

The ink stains on this page are but a testament to the countless drafts I've written, each one a feeble attempt to capture the depth of my emotions, the sincerity of my remorse, and the unwavering strength of my commitment to your safety.

You may find this difficult to believe, but I am a man who has neglected everything around me. I had my chances and didn't have the courage and confidence to pursue what truly mattered. I failed to appreciate the life I had and lost everything because of it. And the worst part of that loss was losing you.

You see, I have only just become a man. As a new man, I now understand that my decisions have consequences that ripple outward, affecting everyone and everything around me. Had I known that my choices, made from a place of trauma and insecurity, would leave you in the danger you're currently facing, I wouldn't have been so careless with my own life. But please know this, Hope – I accept the responsibility for what I've done. I got you into this mess, and I'm going to spend the rest of my days trying to make it right.

With all my heart,

A man who is finally learning to believe his own dreams

CHAPTER SEVENTEEN

Fall was in full swing, and my obsession with Hope had taken root deep inside me. She was the one bright spot in the dark, twisted mess my life had become. I couldn't shake the feeling that I was partly to blame for where she was now. Despite everything—jail, drug addiction, curses, being stalked and manipulated by her ex—she still managed to show kindness, resilience, and beauty. Somehow, she had held on to her softness. I found myself dreaming about her, about having someone like her in my life. She was the one who inspired me to be better, to help people, to actually feel good about doing good.

I was gone, y'all. Days blurred together as I sat on that rooftop, forgetting the whole point of finding Osiris and experimenting with that cursed cologne and wicked vial. I should've been trying to figure out what else they could do, but I was too caught up in stalking her, just like Naz had done proudly for years.

I started sending her anonymous letters—love notes with little reminders of moments only she and the real Walter would remember. I saw her face light up with confusion and a flicker of recognition every time she found one and read it. She kept those letters secret from Naz, never turning them in to the cops. Perhaps she still harbored a soft spot for Naz in her heart, or maybe she genuinely felt a connection to my spirit, regardless of the form I had assumed.

Naz's behavior kept getting worse. I watched him tear apart the apartment, searching for that missing bottle of cologne. He became more controlling, verbally abusive, lashing out at Hope and accusing her of stealing his stuff. He was nothing without that cologne. I realized it didn't just expose our insecurities; it made us face them. But Naz had done too many horrible things to deal with himself, so he took it all out on Hope. Seeing him treat her like she was nothing fueled my determination. I used his behavior against him, reminding her that better days were ahead.

Sometimes, I'd swipe flowers from Washington Park and leave them in her mailbox, addressed to Ruth, along with a note of love and hope. I wanted her to know someone cared, that someone remembered the good times. I wanted to show her that the man she had once fallen for still existed somewhere. I'd catch her looking out the window after reading my notes, or checking the mailbox, searching for the next edition. I found myself writing every kind thought and gesture I could think of and sharing them with her. I wrote on whatever I could find—cardboard, junk mail, small business flyers, litter.

I became a shadow, haunting her days with whispers of affection penned in red ink—the only writing utensil I could find. Watching her eyes light up as she read my words, unaware of the heart that beat behind them, was the best part. Each letter was a piece of my soul, laid bare on the page, a testament to the love I felt but couldn't claim. I wrote about her beauty, her heterochromia that made her eyes a mesmerizing mystery, her love for fine art that spoke of a deep, sensitive soul. I wrote of her strength, her powerful softness—a paradox that made her all the more enchanting. Every day, I watched her smile as she read the romantic letters from her anonymous admirer.

But then my pen ran dry. Days passed without me leaving any messages, and I saw the disappointment in her eyes when she searched in the usual spots and found nothing. It pained me. I had to do something. So, I approached her, catching her outside our sanctuary, hunting for traces of my love that no longer existed. I measured my steps, my heart pounding in my chest. Then, her scream pierced the air, shattering the silence, and I had to react.

"Quiet, Hope," I urged, my voice low, as I covered her

mouth with my hand, muffling her protests. I had to drag her to the alley, shadows dancing around us. I made sure we were alone before I released her, my palms raised in submission, took a couple steps away to let her know she was safe.

"Listen to me," I pleaded, the words tumbling from my lips like a desperate prayer. "Walter isn't who you think he is. He's hiding something, something dangerous."

She eyed me warily, suspicion etched into every line of her face. But she still listened, and I seized the opportunity to speak, to weave a tapestry of words that spoke to her soul.

"You're more than just a pretty face, Hope," I said, my voice soft with sincerity as I recited a few lines from the letters I'd written. "You're a work of art, a masterpiece waiting to be discovered. And I see you, I see the fire in your eyes, the passion in your heart."

"So, you're the one who's been writing those love notes." Hope's voice was a mix of realization and disappointment. "I knew it."

The wind picked up, carrying with it the distant sound of traffic and the faint aroma of the Thai restaurant around the corner, one of my favorite alleys to eat behind. Hope shivered, whether from the cold or from fear, I couldn't tell.

I wanted to tell her the truth, that I was Walter inside of Naz's body, to lay it all out right then and there, but I knew she wasn't ready to believe me. Not yet.

"Yes, I wrote those letters. Would've written a lot more, but my pen ran out of ink."

Hope's eyes narrowed, her voice laced with skepticism and a hint of anger. "When did you become so artistic? Where'd you learn all those big words?"

"I, I—"

"When did you start paying attention to me?" She continued, frustration growing with each word. "Before, it was all about you, and your drugs, and your boxing career. All the time we were together, I felt like you didn't even know me."

I smiled, was happy we were having conversation, even if

it stemmed from her doubt.

"I'm a new person now. I pay attention. The way you love painting, you lose yourself in your art. I know you. The way you change your hair color to match your mood, your strength, your softness, your loyal behavior. It's what makes you so special."

Her eyes widened in surprise. "You know all of that because you're a crazy stalker. Probably read through my diary or something." She began backing away, calmly, as if she hoped I wouldn't notice.

I grabbed her hand, gently, those large, crusty borrowed hands that once were only used to destroy. I took a deep breath and pulled her back toward me. "Yes, I've been watching you, but not as a creep. I wanted to make sure you were safe, to remind you of your worth, to show you that someone cares deeply for you."

Hope's breath hitched, her eyes searching mine. I could see the internal struggle playing out on her face. "Why?" she whispered, her voice barely audible over the distant hum of the city. "Why now? After everything..."

Shock and confusion played across her face. I was lost in her eyes, too lost to notice her hand slide into her purse and pull out the old knife I once found in the Caddy. I thought I had her, was conjuring up something smooth and romantic to say until she drove the dull knife into my forearm. I never saw it coming. The glint of rusty steel flashed in the moonlight as the knife found its mark. I staggered but didn't fall, just snatched my hand away, my gaze still locked on hers, unwavering in its intensity.

"You can't control me with your muscles and your lies anymore, Killer Naz," she said.

I challenged her, my voice a low growl, soft but masculine. "You think a little pain will make me run? You don't know me, Hope. You don't know what I'm capable of. I'm done running from love, no matter how much it might hurt me."

She put the knife over my heart, her hand trembling. I ran

my fingers around it, adjusted the aim to the center of my chest. "Do it," I dared her. "I'm down for anything that has to deal with you and my heart."

Her eyes widened in shock, and for a moment, I saw a flicker of recognition. She was beginning to see the truth, to remember the man I used to be. But then she freaked out and ran, her footsteps echoing in the alley. I let her go, watching as she stopped to look back. She noticed I wasn't chasing her, reached inside her purse and dropped a pen on the ground before proceeding inside. A tiny smile tugged at her lips.

Hope disappeared from my view, and the sounds of the city seemed to rush back in—car horns, distant sirens, the bass from a live band that played at Bar Louie. I stood there, blood trickling down my arm, the pen lying on the ground like a promise. A small victory, perhaps, but a victory nonetheless.

CHAPTER EIGHTEEN

After seeing Hope again, something inside me ignited like never before. It was as if a dormant part of my soul had awakened, filling me with a sense of purpose and determination I'd never experienced. The connection between us, even in this borrowed body, felt electric, undeniable. It was more than just attraction or infatuation; it was a profound understanding, a recognition of kindred spirits. Seeing her brought back memories I'd buried deep within, memories of the man I used to be before all of this madness. But now, those memories felt like a lifeline, pulling me back to who I was, or at least who I was trying to be again.

I started being bolder. It was as if Hope's presence gave me the courage to push beyond the limits of sanity. I sent more letters, pouring out my heart with every stroke of the pen, my words dripping with desperation and longing. I wrote things I'd never dared to say out loud, baring my soul on those pages. I broke into her building just to leave more flowers at her door, bright red roses that I'd carefully chosen for their symbolism, along with notes that professed my love in the most dramatic way possible. I'd hover near her door, just out of sight, hoping to catch a glimpse of her reaction when she found my tokens of affection. Each time, my heart raced with a mix of fear and anticipation, my chest tightening as I wondered if today would be the day she'd finally come to me.

One night, in a moment of pure madness, I even sang outside her window, feeling ridiculous but desperate to show her how much I cared. My voice cracked with emotion as I belted out a tune that echoed through the quiet streets. I didn't care about the odd looks from passersby or the whispers of the neighbors. All that mattered was that she heard me, that she understood the depth of my feelings. The cops came, like they always do when someone makes a scene, but this time, I didn't run. I fought them away, pushing them back with a force I didn't know I had, all for her amusement. I wanted to make her smile, to see that little curve of her lips that I'd grown to crave. Every time I found a chance, I took it, no matter the cost. I needed her to see me, to recognize the man inside this stolen skin.

After a while, Hope grew comfortable enough to sneak away to meet me whenever Naz was out. Those stolen moments became the highlights of my days, the only thing that kept me sane in this twisted reality. We walked to a secluded spot along the lakefront, where other couples strolled and talked for long hours. The moonlight reflected off the water, casting a soft glow that seemed to wrap around us, making those moments feel almost magical, like we were the only two people in the world. The breeze off the lake was cool, carrying with it the scent of the water and the distant hum of the city. It was the perfect place for our conversation, the kind of place where truths could be whispered into the night and carried away on the wind.

"There's something very different about you now," Hope said, her eyes searching mine with an intensity that made my heart skip a beat. "Something that reminds me of the old you. And something about Walter... it feels off, like he's not who he says he is." Her words hung in the air between us, heavy with suspicion and confusion.

Taking a deep breath, I decided to tell her the whole truth. The moment I'd been both dreading and longing for had finally arrived. My heart pounded in my chest, each beat reverberating through my body like a drum. I could feel a cold sweat breaking out on my forehead, my hands trembling slightly as I reached for her. "I've been trying to tell you that, waiting for the right moment."

"Tell me what?" Her voice was soft, almost a whisper, but the tension in her tone was palpable.

"Please don't hate me, okay?" I knew that what I was about

to say could destroy everything between us, but I couldn't keep it inside any longer. The weight of the secret had been crushing me, and I couldn't bear it another second.

Hope laughed, but there was a nervousness to it that made my stomach churn. "I already kind of hate you. I honestly don't understand why I'm here, what draws me to reading your letters and watching you risk your life to show your affections. Part of it is cute, part of it is just downright sickening." Her laughter echoed through the still night, but there was no humor in it. It was the kind of laugh that masked fear, the kind that covered up the cracks in her façade.

I laughed along with Hope, the best I could, in a sarcastic tone that barely covered my anxiety. I fanned my shirt to let the cold air cool my sweaty belly and neck, trying to gather the courage to say what needed to be said. "The man you think is Walter is actually Naz. I am Walter, trapped in Naz's body."

Hope laughed again, but this time it was tinged with disbelief. Her smile faltered, and for a moment, I could see the doubt flickering in her eyes. "Be serious. You always playing, Naz." She playfully punched me in the shoulder, but her touch felt different now, less affectionate, more hesitant.

"I'm sorry, Hope." Tears were swelling up in my eyes. I felt them forming from deep in my gut, from the place where all my pain and fear had been festering for months. "Naz found you, saw me with you, and fooled me into drinking some kind of potion that disconnected my spirit from my body." The words spilled out of me, raw and desperate. I couldn't hold back the tears anymore. "Hope, he's pretending to be me. I've been trapped inside his meat suit for more than four months." That's how long it'd been at the time, four long, agonizing months of living in someone else's skin.

Hope loses her shit. The punches on my arm came harder, more violent as emotions progressed. Her fists pounded against me with a force that left me breathless, her rage spilling out in every blow.

"I could just kill you!" She grunted, her voice thick with

anger and betrayal. Her eyes flashed with a fury that reminded me of Crystal, Naz's baby momma who'd attacked me on the street by Rune's gym. The memory of that day flickered through my mind, and I could feel the sting of her nails digging into my flesh all over again. I didn't fight back. I allowed her to release some frustration, let her take out her anger on my face, bruising up Naz's body even more.

My heart shattered for her. She was suffering the most enormous heartbreak of her life, and it was all my fault. But my sorrow quickly turned to rage when she finally broke down into a painful cry, the sound tearing through the night like a wounded animal. I couldn't stand to see her like this, couldn't bear the sight of her tears.

"Where is he, Hope? Where can I find Walter, I mean, Naz?" My voice was low, almost a growl, the anger boiling inside me, threatening to spill over.

"He might be at the bar of a strip club," she said, her voice barely audible through the sobs. I could still hear the heartbreaking pain in her tone, the way her words cracked under the weight of her emotions, uncontrollable tears streaming down her face.

"I'm going to the police," she added, but I shook my head, the thought of involving the authorities sending a chill down my spine.

"They won't believe you, Hope. Just go back home, to Ruth's. Hide out there until all of this is over." My words were harsh, more forceful than I intended, but I needed her to understand. This wasn't something the cops could fix, this was something I had to handle myself.

She nodded, a mix of worry, panic, and fear in her eyes. She slapped me in the face again, harder this time, as if trying to wake herself from this nightmare. Then she hesitated, as if wrestling with a decision, her lips trembling as she struggled to find the words.

Finally, she blurted out, "I'm pregnant, Naz, I mean, Walter." Her voice cracked as she continued, the weight of her confession hanging in the air like a dark cloud. "You need to do something more than whatever you've been doing." The words hit me like a punch to the gut, leaving me breathless and reeling.

The world seemed to stop spinning for a moment. Pregnant. Hope was pregnant. The weight of this revelation crashed over me like a tidal wave, drowning me in a sea of emotions. In that moment, I realized that the stakes had just gotten infinitely higher. This wasn't just about me anymore, or even just about Hope. There was an innocent life involved now, a life that depended on me to set things right.

"Hope, I..." I started, but words failed me. What could I possibly say in the face of this news? Everything I'd planned, everything I thought I knew, shattered in that instant, leaving me grasping for something, anything, to hold onto.

She hurried to her car, a small Saturn that seemed to blend into the darkness, leaving me out there on the lakefront, my mind reeling from everything that had just transpired. I watched her taillights disappear into the night, my heart pounding in my chest, my thoughts spinning out of control.

As I watched her drive away, I was overwhelmed by a torrent of emotions. The relief of finally telling Hope the truth was overshadowed by the guilt of not having found a way to tell her sooner. I wondered if she truly believed me, if she could find a way to trust me after all of this.

Having this conversation, as necessary as it was, had been one of the hardest things I'd ever done. The pain of seeing Hope's world shatter, of being the one to deliver such devastating news, was almost unbearable. But I knew it had to be done. Sometimes, the hardest conversations are the most important ones, even when they hurt like hell.

PART THREE

SHADOWS OF THE SELF

February 3, 2003

To the woman who sees beyond appearances,

I write this letter with trembling hands and a heavy heart, hoping that my words can bridge the chasm that has grown between us.

Hope,

The weight of my actions, of my deceptions, sits upon my chest like an immovable stone. Each breath I take reminds me of the pain I've caused you, the trust I've shattered. I find myself drowning in a sea of regret, grasping for the right words to express the depth of my remorse.

I've realized, far too late, that in my desperate attempt to protect you, to reclaim what was stolen from me, I've committed the very sin I accused Naz of – I've deceived you. I've manipulated your emotions, played with your trust, all under the guise of love and protection. The irony of this is not lost on me, and it fills me with a shame so profound I can barely face myself in the mirror.

But Hope, please know this – every word of love I've written, every gesture of affection, every moment we've shared, has been genuine. The man inside this borrowed skin loves you with an intensity that frightens me. It's this love that drove me to such desperate measures, and it's this same love that now compels me to bare my soul to you, to beg for your forgiveness.

I understand if you can't forgive me. I understand if you never want to see me again. But I promise you this – I will do everything in my power to make things right. For you, for our child, for the future we could have had.

I am a man learning to see beyond his own pain, beyond his own desires. I'm learning, too late perhaps, that true love is not about possession or control, but about trust, honesty, and sacrifice. I failed you in all these aspects, and for that, I am truly sorry.

You deserve better than this, Hope. You deserve a love that doesn't come with conditions or deceptions. You deserve a man who can stand tall in his own skin, not one hiding in another's body. I hope, someday, I can be that man for you. But for now, all

I can offer is my sincere apology and a promise to do better.

With all my heart, and all my regrets,

A man still learning the true meaning of love

CHAPTER NINETEEN

Fatigue clung to me like a second skin, but I didn't care—I was beyond caring. My feet pounded the pavement, each step a vow, each breath a prayer that the madness would end as I tore through the city's underbelly like a man possessed.

I stalked the city on foot, cutting through the night like a shadow with weight. The El trains were my arteries, pumping me from one end of the city to the other. Red Line, Blue, Orange, Brown, Green—I rode them all, jumping from the South Side to the North, cutting east, then back out south. I didn't bother paying at the stations; just hopped the turnstiles, slipping past attendants who didn't dare make eye contact, let alone stop me. Seven feet of raw muscle and rage, I cleared paths just by existing—people moved out of my way without a word, fear in their eyes. I was becoming what I was chasing, moving with the same cold, relentless energy as Naz himself. But even with that fire burning through me, he was nowhere to be found. None of the spots Hope suggested turned up a trace of him.

I hit every strip club worth mentioning, each one more garish than the last. I didn't waste time with front doors, just slipped through the kitchen entrances where the stench of grease and stale beer clung to the air like a bad memory. The people in the back didn't bat an eye, too caught up in their own misery, too used to the shadows that slithered through those places. The bouncers stayed up front, guarding the money-makers, oblivious to the storm creeping in. By the time they even noticed me, I'd already scanned the room, eyes slicing through the dim light, hunting for the one face that could set this all right. But every time, I walked out empty-handed.

If I wanted to find Naz, I had to think like Naz, which led me to the darkest corners of the city. The places most folks avoided—the drug alleys where junkies traded their last shred of dignity for a hit; the hoe strolls where broken women sold what little they had left to survive; Cabrini-Green's decaying towers, the Henry Horner Homes, and the Robert Taylor Homes too. Found myself in the grimiest pool halls and underground gambling bars in the depths of neighborhoods like Garfield Park, and Lawndale, where the dice and moods shared the same unpredictable flow. It was in one of these places, a forgotten alley somewhere in Englewood, nestled between abandoned buildings covered in graffiti, that I found a familiar face.

Osiris.

He was leaning against a crumbling wall, a fire burning in a rusty garbage can, casting flickering shadows across the scene. His homies were gathered around, listening as he told a story, his hands gesturing wildly as he described a girl he'd met at some bar. There was something different about him now, a newfound confidence that hadn't been there before. He stood tall, a cocky smile on his lips, his posture screaming victory. He didn't need to reek of that sweaty cologne for me to know it had its claws in him.

"Osiris," I called out, my voice low and tired, trying not to spook the six or seven men who were likely packing heat.

He spun around, eyes wide with recognition. In a flash, he had his gun out, the barrel pointed straight at my chest, his lips curling into a sneer. "Stay back, you ugly-ass My Pet Monster," he spat, humor lacing his threat.

I raised my hands slowly, showing him I meant no harm. "I just want to talk. About the cologne."

Osiris's eyes narrowed, suspicion cutting through the haze of bravado. "What about it? You want it back? Tough luck, big man. This stuff's mine now."

"You don't understand," I said, my voice thick with the urgency he couldn't see. "It's dangerous. It has consequences."

A cruel laugh escaped his lips, echoing off the graffiti-covered walls. "Consequences? Man, the only consequence

I've seen is that I'm finally getting what I deserve." He gestured to himself with a flourish.

I took a step forward, the weight of my words dragging me down. "Listen to me, Osiris. That cologne, it's not what you think. It's—"

The sharp click of the gun's hammer cut me off. Osiris stepped closer, his eyes cold and steady, making it clear he wouldn't miss if he wanted to make a hole. "The police hear so many gunshots in this neighborhood, they don't even blink. I could end you right here, and no one would come looking," he snarled, his voice dripping with venom, yet eerily calm, like he was stating a simple fact. He glanced at his homies, then back at me, a twisted smile playing on his lips. "But I'm not gonna shoot you—I'm having a good day. Now get the fuck on, before I change my mind."

My fists clenched, nails digging into my palms as the frustration rose, nearly breaking free. But this wasn't the place to lose control—not with him standing there, gun in hand. My gaze flicked to the cologne bottle tucked in his jacket, a reminder of what I couldn't afford to lose. I turned on my heel, each step feeling heavier as I walked away, the sound of his laughter echoing behind me, cold and final, like a blade pressing against my throat.

The cologne was out there, being used, twisted into something dangerous. And I had no idea how to stop it. I still feel partly responsible.

I dragged on, though. Dragged myself off the Red Line at 55th Street around the same time dawn had broken over the city. Exhaustion weighed me down, each step heavier than the last, as if the pavement itself was trying to swallow me whole. My feet moved on instinct, leading me back to the rooftop, back around the way to check on Hope, maybe rest this heavy body. But as I trudged forward, something else cut through the haze—the distant toll of church bells, soft yet persistent, calling out to me from a few blocks away.

I obeyed.

The old stone church, its spire stabbing the sky, a Chi-Town historical landmark doomed to be demolished, likely replaced by a strip mall or grocery store. The heavy wooden doors groaned as I pushed them apart, a rush of incense and old hymnals flooding my senses. Inside, the air was thick with silence, broken only by the soft murmur of prayer.

And there he was—Naz. Kneeling at the altar, head bowed like a man seeking redemption.

My breath hitched, heart thudding in my chest. I crept closer, each step a tug-of-war between the need to destroy him and the weight of holding back enough to get my body back in one piece. Every instinct screamed to rush him, to drag him off the pulpit, maybe even snap his spine over a pew, but I held back, keeping myself in check. My heart pounded so fiercely, I was sure he could feel the tremors in the stillness between us.

Naz was oblivious, lost in his own twisted prayer. "Lord," he whispered, my voice cracking with emotion, sounding foreign even to my own ears. "I know I've done wrong, but I'm trying to be better. Help me keep Hope. She argues with me, she doesn't do what I say, she doesn't understand what's best for her." His voice wavered, fingers locked, tears streaming down his face like he believed every ignorant word he was saying. "Lord, please give me the strength to guide her, to control her if I must. Without the cologne, I feel so weak. I need your power to make her see that I'm what she needs. Help me be the man who can keep her in line, who can give her the life she deserves, even if she doesn't know it yet."

For a moment, his raw desperation hit me, and I saw Naz not as the monster who had stolen my life, but as a broken man, clinging to a fucked-up version of love like most people today, a love as distant from reality as the moon from the earth. But just as quickly, the illusion shattered, leaving only the rage. If Naz had truly loved Hope the way he thought he did, he'd let her be free—to bring light into a world he had only filled with ugliness and chaos.

"He can't help you control her," I laughed, my voice invading the sanctuary silence. "God actually cares about how people feel."

Naz jumped, startled, spinning around to face me. His eyes—my eyes—were wide with shock and fear, like he thought God himself had spoken back. "Walter," he breathed, scrambling to his feet, the fear in his voice palpable. He looked around the empty church, realized he was alone with a giant, smelly, musclebound brute with nothing but red in his eyes. I could see it in the way the sweat started to bead on his forehead—how the tables had turned, and the fear was now his to carry.

"Does it matter?" I took a step closer, fists clenched at my sides, every muscle in my body screaming for action. The urge to lash out, to make him pay for everything he'd done, was almost overwhelming. "What matters is that this ends now. Tell me how to switch back. Tell me how to undo what you've done."

"Walter, I'm so sorry," he choked out, his voice breaking under the weight of his fear. He grabbed the large Bible from the altar, clutching it like a shield against the storm he knew was coming. "I never meant for it to go this far."

I hesitated, thrown off by his sudden humility. My eyes drifted to the statue of the man on the cross above us. I thought, maybe Naz had enough sense to kneel and be respectful to him. After all, we were in a church.

"I know how to fix this," Naz said, standing hunched over, wiping tears from his eyes with his sleeve.

"You lie in the house of the lord," I said. "I just heard you tell God that you don't have the cologne."

His gaze drifted to the cross, lingering on the nail piercing the feet, before returning to me. In that moment, I saw myself reflected back—my own sincere eyes and worried brow. I saw a lost boy struggling to understand the world he was thrown in. My own pitiful figure, the way I must've looked when I bumped into Naz in the park, folding like a coward and fleeing. I saw that same weakness in myself when I left Hope standing alone on the curb. The image was revolting, filled me with shame and pity. I vowed to never sink to such a low again.

"We need to drink the holy water together," Naz said, his voice tinged with desperation. "It's the only way to reverse the switch."

Suspicion gnawed at me, but a dangerous, tempting hope began to blossom in my chest. "Why should I trust you?"

Naz sighed, still hiding himself behind the large bible. "Hope doesn't really love me; she thinks I'm you. I only meant to see her one last time, to hold her again, to feel the way she looks at me and makes me feel strong. What was supposed to be one day turned into months, and here we are."

His words rang with a sincerity that was hard to ignore, but I had to remind myself that I wasn't staring into a mirror. I was looking at Naz—the man who'd killed his own grandmother, the woman who'd cared for him after his Pops died in jail and his mom fell victim to the same damn drugs that had locked his father away. I was talking to the man who double-crossed Rune, who stepped into a role meant to teach him the value of discipline and integrity but used those skills for deceit and destruction.

"No," I said, my voice cutting through the air like a blade. "You don't get to play the victim here. You don't get to stand in front of me and act like you're the one who's been wronged. You took something from me that I'll never get back, and you've hurt people who never deserved it. I don't know if this holy water trick will fix anything, but I know one thing— you're not getting off that easy."

I saw a flicker of hesitation in his eyes. "I'm tired, Walter. Tired of running, tired of lying. I want my life back. I have a lot of unfinished business."

"Unfinished business?" I spat, stepping closer, my anger bubbling over. "You think this is some unfinished business? You think you can waltz back into my life and clean up your mess? You've got a lot to answer for, and I'm not about to let you off the hook just because you're tired. If you really want redemption, then you better start showing me more than just tears and apologies."

Naz approached the fountain of holy water, which sat two steps above where I stood, surrounded by arrangements of red, black, and green candles. A few ornate cups and other religious items were placed reverently around it, giving the scene an almost sacred air. He dipped one of the cups into the water, his hands trembling as he raised it to his lips and drank. For a moment, nothing happened. Then his face twisted in agony.

"Ahhhh!" Naz cringed, dropping to one knee, clutching the Bible at his side like a lifeline.

"Naz?" I stepped closer, my eyes darting around, searching for the source of his pain.

He doubled over the fountain, gasping. "It burns," he wheezed. "Oh God, it burns."

Was I watching my own body die? My thoughts scrambled,

my mind fogging up in panic. "Man, I knew you were the devil, but I didn't think the holy water would hurt you like this."

For a second, I could've sworn I heard a faint chuckle. I leaned in, peering behind the large Bible, and saw his face, drenched in sweat, twisted in a grimace like a fiend. Through gritted teeth, he managed to speak. "It hurts so bad, Walter."

My confusion spiked, panic setting in. "I'm gonna run and call 911!"

At first, he shouted, "NO!" in a quick panic, his voice cracking with desperation. But the outburst drained him, and his voice quickly faded back to that weak, strained tone, as if even shouting had cost him. "They're gonna lock your ass up," he muttered, barely audible. "Just come and pray with me."

"Pray with you?" I echoed, disbelief and suspicion creeping into my voice.

Naz doubled down, his eyes pleading. "Please. I don't want to die like this."

Reluctantly, I kneeled down just below the fountain of

holy water, directly beside him. I closed my eyes.

The words felt hollow in my mouth, but I pushed through, desperate for anything to work. I focused on the prayer, clinging to the hope that it might somehow set things right, that it might return me to the life I had, to Hope. I was so consumed by it all, so lost in the rhythm of the words, that I didn't notice when Naz's labored breathing stopped.

I turned just in time to see the large Bible slam into my face. The impact sent me reeling, my head cracking against the cold, unforgiving floor. Stars burst in my vision as I crumpled to the ground, pain radiating from the back of my skull. Everything started to fade to black, but through the haze, I caught a glimpse of Naz standing over me, a sick grin plastered on his face. Then I watched him bolt out of the church, laughing, as the darkness swallowed me whole.

CHAPTER TWENTY

I opened my eyes to the same door Naz had run out of, still lying in the very position he'd left me in, sprawled out on the floor near the altar, beneath the fountain of holy water. I couldn't move—Naz's body felt heavy, unresponsive, like I'd woken up in that garbage can all over again. My spirit was awake, but my body seemed stuck, disconnected, struggling to load back into reality. Fear gnawed at me, anger simmering beneath the surface for falling into Naz's trap yet again. I tried to turn my neck, to move even a finger, but I was paralyzed. Maybe it was shock, or something else—something strange and invisible, forcing me to face the front door.

The doors creaked open, and daylight flooded in, only to be swallowed by the shadow of an older man as he stepped inside and closed them behind him.

He was an elderly Black man with nappy gray locs and patches of a scruffed-up sandy gray beard. Dressed in olive green Dickies, pants and shirt, with worn work boots—he looked like a soldier from some forgotten war, strong enough to sweep the church but maybe not strong enough to carry a full bucket of water. He held a broom and dustpan, moving with a deliberate, unhurried pace.

I couldn't move my mouth to call out, so I watched, helpless, as he slowly swept his way down the middle aisle. He approached the altar, his gaze sweeping over the floor until it landed on me, lying there like discarded trash beneath the holy water fountain—limp, head tilted, legs and arms splayed out. His nose wrinkled as he caught the scent of sweat and blood, likely thinking I was dead at first.

But it was his eyes that sent chills through me. There was something in the way he looked at me, something that sparked life back into every nerve in my body. Suddenly, I could move my neck, just enough to follow his movements as he walked around me, methodically filling the same cup Naz had drunk from. Without a word, he poured the holy water over my face, almost drowning me as I coughed and sputtered, jolting back into reality.

"It's a beautiful day, young man, almost two in the afternoon. It would be a great sin for you to miss too much more of it."

The old man's voice was smooth yet powerful, carrying the weight of a seasoned jazz singer's melody. It was as if my ears were connected directly to his voice box; I was sure I could have heard that strong, smooth whisper from the opposite side of the church.

He dipped the cup into the fountain again, then carefully handed it to me, offering it as though it held something more than just water.

I sat up slowly, feeling the water he'd already poured on my face drip to the floor. The cup felt cool in my hands, a chill that seemed out of place, but I didn't question it. Somehow, it all made sense at the time.

After a tentative sip, I looked up at the man's gentle smile before gulping the rest. The coldness spread through me, searching Naz's body until it found me. For the first time in months, I felt clear—truly clear.

The old man leaned on his broom in a way that defied logic, balancing his entire weight on the slim handle with the ease of a master. I started to think he was some sort of retired guru, shaman, or sensei—someone who knew things that couldn't be learned from any books.

"How'd you get here, young man?" he asked.

I hesitated, then began, "Well, there's this guy who might be my cousin, and he keeps lying and stealing and doing bad things to people. He—"

The old man silenced me with a simple lift of his hand from the broom. There was something in the way he pointed two fingers in the air without extending his arm, a slight tilt of his head, and that same calm smile. It compelled me to stop talking.

"No," he said, his voice still smooth but now, a powerful sternness, one that struck me like thunder. "I didn't ask you about anyone else." He continued. "I asked, why are *YOU* here?"

His words hit me hard. For so long, I'd been focused on Naz—on his lies, his betrayals, his darkness. But in that moment, I realized I'd never truly confronted the darkness within myself, the choices that had led me to this point, the cowardice that had driven me to such lows.

I lowered my head, shame washing over me like a wave. The old man stood upright, bringing the tip of his broom gently to my chin, lifting my face so I had no choice but to meet his eyes. The intensity in those eyes was overwhelming, pulling out emotions I had buried deep, words I had been too afraid to say. And in that moment, I broke. Tears streamed down my face. His gaze made me spill everything I'd been holding back, a release that felt like the first step toward becoming someone new.

"I... I guess it's because I've always been a coward," I finally confessed, the words spilling out like a dam had burst. "Always looking for a way out, running from my problems, or looking for someone else to fix them, using things outside of myself to fill empty spaces inside."

The tears flowed freely down my face, and through the blur of them, I saw him smiling—a soft, proud smile that made me cry even harder. He didn't say a word at first, just stood there, holding that broom like it was the most natural thing in the world.

"Was that so bad?" He finally asked, his voice steady and warm. "Owning up to your mess? Was that so bad?"

I shook my head, the broom still holding my chin up, preventing me from hiding from the truth. Then, he slowly removed the broom, and I expected my head to drop, but it didn't. My head stayed up, my gaze steady. I felt clear, as if I'd drunk the holy water all over again. The fear was still there, but I respected it. A strange sense of liberation, made me feel unstoppable, like the fear could now be used like the compass in my backpack of homeless essentials.

"I am also neglectful," I confessed, the words tumbling out of me. "I didn't appreciate the life I had. I'd see people walking around with their families, everyone with somebody, and I felt so damn lonely. Alone my whole life."

The old man nodded, his smile widening just a bit. "Now you're getting the hang of it," he said, his voice like a gentle push forward. "Get it all off your chest, young man. Face yourself like a man."

His words were both a challenge and a comfort, urging me to dig deeper, to unearth the parts of myself I'd buried beneath layers of blame and denial.

"I'm stupid for trusting people I shouldn't," I confessed, the words spilling out before I could stop them.

The old man chuckled softly, shaking his head. "Whoa,

whoa… slow down, young man. Seems you've gone a bit too far."

He walked over and sat beside me, the air around him seeming to hum with a quiet energy. The hairs on my arms stood on end, like they were reaching for him. I straightened up, my posture instinctively adjusting under his steady gaze.

"I've seen a lot of hard men come through these doors, searching for answers," he began, his voice low and resonant. "Men who could spit into a pot ten yards away without jerking their necks. Men who would snarl at a little baby girl if it made them feel the slightest bit of softness. You know why they're so hard? Because they're scared."

His words hung in the air, sinking deep into my chest.

"Everyone's afraid these days. Scared to trust, scared to love, scared to show respect or kindness because they think it makes them weak. They're stuck, always on edge, always trying to be tougher than the tough world they think they see around them. They look at each other with frowns when they really want to show love, thinking it is keeping them safe, but it's more of a prison."

He paused, letting his words settle, then continued, "Being brave enough to trust someone doesn't make you stupid. It makes you beautiful. It takes real courage to stick your neck out, to believe in someone or something when there's a chance you could get hurt. That's not weakness—that's strength. The kind of strength that comes from being open, from being willing to connect, even when it's scary."

He leaned in a little closer, his eyes boring into mine. "Unfortunately, there will always be people in this world who overreact to their fears. People who step on flowers, destroy art, and laugh at others when they're at their most vulnerable. But remember, that's not on you—that's on them. The brave are the ones who make sure they aren't part of the problem."

The old man paused for a moment, as if catching himself, the words seeming to stir something deep within him. It was as if the truth he was speaking was so powerful, even he had to take a breath.

"And searching for purpose, trying to understand your past and what it means for your future—those are also things that brave men do. It doesn't matter how hard or soft they may look on the outside. The real battle is inside, and it's the men who face that battle who are the strongest."

His words struck a chord deep within me, resonating with truths I'd been too afraid to acknowledge. Trust, love, self-expression—these weren't weaknesses. They were the hardest battles of all, requiring a kind of bravery that went far beyond physical toughness.

I slowly stood up, feeling a strange sense of lightness, like a weight had been lifted off my shoulders. The old man continued to smile, as if it were the only thing his face knew to do, his eyes still filled with warmth, as if it were the only way he knew to see the world.

"Thank you," I managed to say, my voice thick with emotion. The old man just nodded, as if he knew exactly what

I meant, even though I couldn't fully express it.

I turned to leave, glanced down the aisle and towards the door. Then the man stepped behind, said, "Good luck, Walter. I'll be rooting for you every step of the way."

I froze. My heart skipped a beat. I hadn't told him my name. I turned back around, a thousand questions swirling in my mind. But the old man was gone. The church was empty, the only sound the distant hum of the city outside.

CHAPTER TWENTY ONE

The police on patrol were getting busier. With calls on the rise in that district, Hope's protection grew slimmer and slimmer. What started as one car parked all day dwindled to them only driving by to check in from time to time. By then, it was easier for me to slip in and out of my building, easier to break in the back door, creep up the back stairs, and knock on Ruth's door.

I saw Ruth's shadow through the window. She peeped through to see it was me, then opened the door slightly, leaving the chain locked between us.

"Who are you?" she demanded, her voice sharp and defensive, but then her eyes zeroed in on my face, and her expression twisted with alarm. "What the hell happen to your eye?"

"It's nothing," I muttered, trying to dismiss her concern. "Got hit with a Bible. Long story."

Ruth stared at me, the shock still evident in her eyes. "Look like you been through hell," she said, her voice softer but still laced with disbelief.

"It's nothing I can't handle," I replied, forcing a weak smile. "Just let me in, okay?"

"Wait just a minute." Ruth raised her hand like a stop sign, stamping it directly in front of me. Then she leaned in close to my good eye, searching my face as if she were trying to see through me. "So, are you really Walter in there? How do I know it's you?"

"Yes, it's me," I said, holding my head up, trying to look proud despite how grotesque I must have felt, looked, or even smelled at the time. "The boy from down the hall."

Ruth glanced behind me, making sure the coast was clear. Her eyes darted back to me, and she reminded me to look too.

"Just let me in," I said again, trying to sound more confident.

"Wait!" she insisted, her voice firm. "If you Walter, tell me, how you like your coffee?"

I blinked, momentarily thrown off balance. "I... I've never had coffee. Just one disgusting sip when you offered me some when we first met, remember?"

Her gaze didn't soften, still scrutinizing me. "And why were you hiding from us after that first meeting?"

Shame washed over me, heavy and cold, as the memory surfaced. "I wasn't hiding," I muttered, the truth raw on my tongue. "I was ashamed. I felt like a burden."

A twitch played at the corner of Ruth's lips, a flicker of something close to empathy, but she didn't let her guard down. "One last question," she said, her tone laced with a dark amusement. "Are you a male prostitute?"

A laugh bubbled up from deep within me, despite the gravity of the situation. "No, Ruth. You thought that because of all the women coming and going from my apartment."

Ruth's eyes studied me for a long moment before she finally sighed, the tension in her shoulders easing slightly. "Okay," she said, unlocking the chain. "Come in." She stepped aside, and I crossed the threshold into warmth and familiarity. "Hope told me everything," she said. "I didn't want to believe it, but... come in."

For the first time, I noticed the gentle swell of her belly, the unmistakable curve of life growing strong within her. It was a sight so pure, so magical, that it momentarily eclipsed the fear etched on her face. In that moment, I saw not just the woman I loved, but the quiet miracle unfolding within her—a beauty that should have been celebrated, yet was clouded by the shadows of all the bullshit she had to endure.

"You look terrible," she said, her voice softer than I'd expected. Her gaze lingered on my swollen eye and ragged clothes. "There are clean clothes in the bathroom. And food." She paused, then added, "You should shower first. I'll bring you some ice for that eye."

The hot water was a baptism, washing weeks of grime and despair from my skin. For a fleeting moment, I could almost believe that everything that had happened was just a nightmare, that I could wake up and find myself whole again. But as I wiped the steam from the mirror, reality hit hard. My eye—swollen, bruised, and sickly yellow around the edges— was a grotesque reminder of everything I'd been through. The skin was stretched tight, red, and angry, with the lid nearly sealed shut. A dark bruise had spread, with a crusted cut beneath my eyebrow where the Bible had struck. It was an ugly, painful mess, and the sight of it made me wince.

Before I could process the eye any further, the bathroom door burst open, jarring me from my thoughts. Hope and Ruth both rushed in, both their faces twisted in panic. "Shh," Hope hissed. "Naz is here! He's knocking on the door."

I quickly grabbed for my towel, covering myself before turning to Ruth. "Let that motherfucker in, and I'll grab him, tie him up, and we can torture his ass," I said, a greedy excitement tingling in my veins.

"Not up in here!" Ruth snapped, her voice firm. "You not bringing bad shit up in here!"

Without missing a beat, Ruth stripped off her clothes right in front of me, turned the shower back on to wet her hair, and cranked up the heat to let the steam rise and fill up the bathroom. In one swift motion, she snatched the towel from around me, leaving me standing there, and marched out of the bathroom, leaving the door slightly ajar behind her. By then, Naz's soft knocks had escalated into loud, desperate bangs.

"Wait just a damn minute," Ruth yelled, opening the front door just enough for him to see her wet hair and bathrobe through the narrow view the chain lock allowed. "Can a girl take a shower?" she added, her voice dripping with irritation.

"Have you seen Hope?" Naz's voice, distorted yet undeniably mine, was thick with desperation.

"Not since she moved in with you," Ruth lied smoothly, her voice a shield. "Me and her had a fight. I told her not to come back."

"But I need to find her," Naz's voice cracked, revealing just how lost he was. "I've been drinking, I haven't eaten... I'm lost without her."

Ruth's tone shifted, hardening. "How do you like your coffee, Walter?"

A pause. "What? I... uh, black? Why?"

"And why were you hiding from us after we first met?"

"I wasn't... what are you talking about?"

Naz's confusion hung heavy in the air, almost tangible. "Look, can I come in? Maybe you can help me find her." He peered over Ruth's shoulder, his eyes darting through the apartment. The sound of the shower still running and the steam pouring out didn't escape him.

"I just want to finish my bath so I can put up my feet and watch *Girlfriends*," Ruth said, her voice strained as she struggled to hold both the door and the lie shut.

"Please, I just need someone smart to talk to," Naz

insisted, his desperation clawing its way to the surface. Then, the unmistakable sound of a scuffle.

"No!" Ruth's voice rang out, fierce and unyielding. "You need to leave. Now!"

I stuck my head out of the bathroom, ready to jump in if Ruth needed me. I watched her slam the door shut, then peer through the peephole to watch Naz's walk of shame down the hall. When I heard the door to unit 7D slam shut, Ruth finally turned around, her back against the door. She slid down to the floor, releasing a hard breath like she'd been holding it too long.

"Damn. That was fun," she said, a crooked grin breaking through her exhaustion.

I went back into the bathroom and dressed quickly, the weight of exhaustion heavy on my shoulders. I emerged to grab a bite, but the sight of my face in the newspaper made my stomach drop. I tossed it in the trash, trying to ignore the gnawing sense of dread.

Ruth turned on the TV, and the room was soon filled with the harsh reality of a special news report. My face stared back at me, the word "WANTED" glaring above it. The charges scrolled beneath: home invasion, theft, indecent exposure, assault with a blunt object, stalking, and—worst of all—the murder of Nona Lacoste.

Hope's eyes widened with fear as she took in the news. "That poor old woman. She was so sweet," she said, her voice trembling. "Naz... he's completely lost it."

The weight of it all crashed down on me. This wasn't just about getting my body back anymore. It was about stopping a monster—a monster wearing my face.

Hope broke the silence, her voice cutting through the tension like a knife. "You need to see Sage. You told me he's the oldest living person who's used that cologne. He'll have answers."

I felt my chest tighten at the mention of Sage's name. "I... I can't," I stammered. "Last time... it was too much. I can't face him again."

Hope's hand found mine, her touch grounding me in the chaos. "I know you're scared, Walter. But running from Sage is running from yourself. We need to do this."

Her words pierced through the fog of my fear, pulling me back to that dark church, to the old man's intense gaze and his cryptic warning about facing my true self. I could almost hear his voice again, urging me to confront the inner battles I'd been avoiding.

I took a deep breath, the weight of his words settling heavily on my shoulders. "Okay," I said finally, the resolve firming in my voice. "Let's go."

Ruth jumped up from her chair, grabbed her car keys. Said, "Finally, some action."

Ruth's light blue '94 Dodge Caravan was an old clunker, with the sliding doors stuck tight. So, I had to climb in through the front, awkwardly squeezing my way to the back. Once I managed it, I had plenty of room to stretch out, thanks to the missing chairs.

"What are you looking at?" Ruth shot back, a defensive edge in her tone. "You could fit more groceries in here like that."

I chuckled despite myself.

"It's not funny," Ruth continued, her voice a mix of frustration and amusement. "You could have used it for work. Could have bring your clients in there, back before you lose yourself." She laughed. Hope laughed. I most definitely did not.

We arrived at the mental institution, and my face was plastered everywhere—posters, notices, warnings. I couldn't risk going in, so I handed Hope and Ruth a list of questions to ask Sage themselves, hoping they'd find something useful.

After an hour and a half of waiting, the two women returned, their faces etched with frustration. "They won't let us in," Ruth said, her voice heavy with defeat. "We tried everything. Showed them every ID we had, spoke to four different people. They all said the same thing—Sage is too dangerous, and they can't risk it."

"Then we find another way," I said.

We regrouped in the minivan, quickly hatching a plan to return under the cover of night. Once we arrived, I found an unguarded back entrance by the trash area—the most overlooked spot in any large facility.

Inside, I navigated through the dimly lit hallways to the medical office, where I rifled through files until I located Sage's. The documents—court records, therapist notes, police files—painted a picture of a deeply troubled life, and I also discovered files on Melvin and Slim, detailing their various offenses.

I noted Sage's room number, stuffed the folder into my pants, and made my way through the eerily silent corridors. Standing outside his door, I peered through the small observation window and saw Sage sitting in his room, staring through the skylight, rocking back and forth, moaning Laura's name at the moon.

"Sage?" I called softly. No response.

I took a deep breath. "I... I wish things could have been different between us," I started, the words tumbling out. "I wish we could have had a normal life. You could have been proud of me, you know? Taught me to ride a bike, throw a spiral..."

My voice cracked. "I struggle with my emotions sometimes. Never had a consistent man in my life to show me how to properly use them. That could have been you."

Sage continued rocking, seemingly oblivious to my presence. But I pressed on, pouring out years of pent-up feelings. When I finally fell silent, the weight on my chest felt a little lighter, like I'd sipped that holy water again. I took a long heavy look at the man behind the glass. With a brave heart, I turned and made my way back to the van. Hope and Ruth were waiting, concern etched on their faces, waiting for me to tell an amazing story about breaking inside of this place but I had nothing to say.

In the heavy silence that filled the van, Hope's fingers tightened around my hand, her grip firm and unyielding. I could feel the anger still simmering within her—the fire in her eyes was unmistakable. But her touch spoke of something deeper, something that even her anger couldn't shatter.

"I'm loyal to a fault, you know that," she mumbled to herself, her disappointment just loud enough to hear through the sounds of that old rusty van.

Ruth, sitting in the driver's seat, let out a derisive snort. "Loyal? Or just plain stupid?"

The words hung in the air, heavy with the weight of everything we'd been through. I felt the tension thickening, the pressure of it all threatening to break us down.

"How 'bout this?" I turned to Hope with a small, crooked smile. "I'll give you five good punches to my face, anytime you want, for the rest of your life—just as long as I can still see out of the other eye afterward."

Hope thought about the offer close enough to make me break in a sweat. Her anger cracked just a little, a half smile from the corner of her lips. But the heaviness in her gaze didn't lift. "You'd let me do that?" she asked, her voice softer now, the edge of frustration giving way to something else.

"If it'll make you feel better," I shrugged, "then yeah, I'd take it. I deserve it."

"But why? It wouldn't change anything." Hope

"It might make you feel better," Ruth butted in.

Hope laughed with Ruth at my expense, the tension easing just a little. Then she turned to me, grabbed my face by the chin and spoke to my soul. "Nothing we do now will unmake a choice we have made. All we can do is keep moving forward, more carefully, and learn to live with what we've done—and what's been done around us."

I looked at her, a small, tired smile folding in. "What if we just... forget everything?" My voice was quiet, almost pleading. "What if we just ran away, you and me? We don't need to get my skin back. We could start fresh, somewhere far away from all this."

We gazed into each other, felt the tension easing just a bit by the way she held my hand. For a moment, it felt like the world outside the van didn't matter. It was just the two of us, holding onto whatever hope we had left.

Ruth shook her head, speaking mildly under her breath, "You're both idiots."

* * *

I, Walter Mosley (Patient #3324D), formally acknowledge and apologize for my unauthorized access to the medical and police records of Sage Henry Marshall. I understand the gravity of this breach of confidentiality and take full responsibility for my actions. However, I must stress that this access was crucial to my journey of self-discovery and healing. The contents of these files have provided invaluable insights into my own struggles and those of my family, and possibly a way for me to get out this mess. Allow me to explain:

One note read: *"Patient exhibits deep-seated insecurity. Relies heavily on external validation."* I couldn't help but see myself in those words. How many times had I sought approval from others, never feeling quite good enough on my own? I remembered the foster homes, the constant need to prove myself, to be the perfect child so they wouldn't send me back.

Another entry caught my eye: *"S. expresses regret over the inability to form lasting connections. Fears intimacy due to past betrayals."* The parallels were undeniable. I thought of Hope, of how I'd pushed her away time and time again. The way she'd looked at me with such open trust, and how I'd nearly run away from it.

But it was in those last few pages that truly had me shook: *"Patient's fixation on the cologne appears to be a manifestation of his desire for control. He claims that the substance inside the cologne bottle and the substance inside the vial are the same."*

Reading those words, everything clicked into place. I realized that Naz and I had both drunk the sweaty cologne. The connection between us suddenly became clear. Maybe drinking it again would reverse whatever had happened to us. It was a desperate thought, but it made more sense than the only other option I could think of: beating Naz senseless and running away with Hope. But I pride myself on having self-control. Losing it to violence would be my last resort—the final step toward becoming like Sage, the man who lost his cool and killed his brother. His ending is already made...

I recognize that my actions were unethical and potentially illegal. However, I hope you can understand the desperate circumstances that drove me to this point. My goal was not to violate privacy.

I am prepared to face any consequences for my actions. However, I ask that you consider the therapeutic value of the insights I've gained from these records. They have been instrumental in my progress and in helping me to contextualize my experiences.

Moving forward, I commit to respecting the confidentiality of others and to fixing my bullshit through the appropriate channels.

Thanks. Hoping you understand.
Walter Mosley
Patient #3324D

CHAPTER TWENTY TWO

After poring over Sage's police files and therapy notes, I made my way to the alley where I'd last seen Osiris—the only person I knew who still had the cologne. The stench of decay and desperation hung heavy in the air. My footsteps echoed off the grimy walls, each step pulling me closer to a confrontation I both dreaded and needed.

I found him huddled behind a dumpster, his once-imposing frame now trembling. The effects of the cologne were etched into every single line of his face, every twitch of his fingers.

"Osiris!"

He looked up, and for a moment, I barely recognized him. His eyes were wide and bloodshot, darting in every direction as if searching for something that wasn't there. His skin clung to his bones, giving him a skeletal, fiendish look. He scratched at his arms, twitching like a man on the edge. I knew it wasn't drugs that had done this to him.

"You," he rasped, his voice strained like it hurt him to speak. He turned his back to me, attempting to shield his face and avoid more embarrassment. "What the hell do you want? Come to finish me off?"

I shook my head and took a step closer. The stench of his unwashed body mixed with the unmistakable odor of the cologne made my stomach churn.

"Give it to me. And the vial." I demanded.

Osiris clutched the cologne bottle to his chest. "You can't have it," he hissed through yellowed teeth, spittle flying from his cracked lips. "It's mine! I need it!"

I approached slowly, hands raised. "You don't need the cologne, man, you need help. That stuff's killing you."

He stumbled backward, nearly tripping over his own feet. "No! You don't understand. It's everything. It's... it's..." His words dissolved into incoherent mumbling.

I reached forward, quickly grabbing for the bottle. Despite his weakened state, Osiris fought with the desperate strength of a cornered animal. His filthy nails raked across my arm as we grappled. He even tried to bite me.

"Let go!" I grunted, trying to pry his fingers loose without hurting him.

"Never!" Osiris shrieked, his voice cracking.

With a final twist and pull, I wrenched the cologne free. Osiris's eyes widened in shock, and he let out a guttural scream of rage and frustration. He collapsed to the ground, flailing his arms and kicking his legs in a wild, erratic dance of despair. His body convulsed as he gasped for breath, his movements growing increasingly frenzied. He thrashed about, his voice rising to a high-pitched wail, as if the loss of the cologne was a devastating blow on his life.

"You made me hurt my knee, you bastard," he wheezed, glaring up at me with pure hatred. "Where's my pistol? I'll kill you for this. I swear I'll…"

His threat trailed off into a fit of coughing. I stood there, cologne in hand, watching as this shell of a man curled into himself, shaking and shit.

"Where's the vial?" I asked in a threatening tone.

"Fuck you…" He responded, kept his back to me. "Somebody stole it. Can't trust nobody these days."

The victory felt hollow. Osiris looked so small now, so broken. It was like taking a crack pipe from a family member.

"Sorry, man." I whispered, though I wasn't sure if he could hear me anymore.

As I turned to leave, Osiris's raspy voice stopped me. "I hate you," he croaked. "You musclebound Sean Price-looking motherfucker."

I didn't bother to respond. Osiris was already too far gone, lost in his own despair, so I left him there, huddled in the alley, to figure it out for himself while I made my last dash to Ruth's place.

The cologne was burning a hole in my pocket. Felt it bouncing around in there, taunting me on my jog. Faces and buildings blurred into a chaotic tapestry, while my mind raced with possibilities and fears. What if drinking the cologne doesn't work? What if it made things worse? I needed to see Hope before I did anything—whether it was a farewell or a desperate plea for understanding; I had to explain my plan to her. Beneath the fear and doubt was a current of desperate hope. This had to work. It was my last chance.

Ruth let me in the back door and stumbled her way back to the kitchen table where Hope was sitting. The half-empty tequila bottle and shot glass made it clear Ruth had been drinking heavily. As Ruth reached for another shot, Hope quickly grabbed the shot glass from the table and discreetly tucked it into her pocket. Ruth didn't notice, her focus already drifting. Hope's gesture was deliberate—she needed to cut Ruth off for the night.

"Where my glass?" Ruth asked.

I shrugged my shoulders. "Don't look at me, I just got here."

Hope butted in. "Girly, I think you've had enough."

"Fine!" Ruth slurred, grabbing the Cuervo by the neck. "Don't go trading places now." She pointed her fingers like a gun, gave a tipsy wink, and wobbled away to flop down onto the living room sofa. She left the cap on the table where Hope sat, contemplating her next move.

"Walter, what's going on? Where have you been?" Hope asked, her voice a mixture of relief and suspicion.

I took a deep breath, trying to steady myself. Kneeling down, I grabbed Hope's hand, held it like it was time to pop the big question. "Hope, I think I've found a way to fix this," I said, pulling the cologne from my pocket. "I'm going back to the rooftop to take another shot of this stuff. Maybe… maybe it'll reverse everything."

Her eyes widened as she saw the bottle, her hands instinctively reaching for her belly. "Walter, no. You can't seriously be thinking of doing that again. You don't even know if that will work."

"It's the only clue I found in Sage's files," I replied, feeling the desperation creeping into my voice. "I don't know what's going to happen, but I have to try. It's the only shot I've got left."

Hope shook her head, standing up from her chair. "You're being gullible, Walter. I told you, some choices you can't undo. Don't you see that?"

"We don't have any other options!" I snapped, frustration spilling over. "If I don't try this, then what? We keep running? Hiding? I'm done with that. I want my life back. I want to be normal, start a family with you, buy a house with a white picket fence and a big red door. We could get a poodle, travel, go to our kids' baseball games. We can't do any of that beautiful shit while I'm out on the run, hiding from the law and everyone Naz has ever crossed."

Her expression softened, but there was a steely

determination in her eyes. "Walter, listen to me. I can't lose you. This isn't the answer. Please, don't do this."

I sighed, caught between my love for her and the urgent need to reclaim my life. "Hope, I'm going across the alley, back to the roof. I won't drink it here because I don't know what will happen. But please understand, I'm drinking this for us. If it doesn't work… I want you to know I tried. Don't come looking for me. Hopefully, when I find you again, I'll be back to my normal self."

We argued back and forth, the tension thick in the air, but no boundaries were crossed. Hope's words cut deep, but I was resolute. Finally, she sighed, shaking her head as she stepped closer, wrapping her arms around me in a tight hug. "I see there's no changing your mind. So, please be careful," she whispered, her voice breaking. "I need you."

"That's why I gotta do this." I murmured back, feeling a strange calm wash over me. "I promise, Hope. Everything will be okay for you, with or without me."

After a moment, I pulled away, kissed her forehead, and turned to leave. I felt the weight of the cologne bottle in my pocket, feeling the finality of the decision I was about to make.

Minutes later, I arrived at the rooftop and created a makeshift spiritual ambiance using borrowed cinnamon and clove candles from Ruth. In between the flickering candles, legs folded, I sat, attempting to uphold some semblance of ritual. I reached into my pocket, fumbled for the cologne, and pulled out Ruth's shot glass instead—the one Hope had hidden. The cologne bottle was missing. Panic surged through me as I scrambled through my other pockets. It wasn't there.

"Fuckkkk!" I screamed, startling the pigeons and sending them flapping away in a frenzy.

Then it hit me—Hope had tricked me, trying to save me from myself.

I grabbed my fake binoculars and scanned Ruth's window. She was passed out on the couch, but Hope was nowhere in sight. I shifted my gaze to unit 7D, and there she was. Even from a distance, I could see how the past months had worn her down. Her shoulders slumped under the weight of exhaustion, her movements slow and labored. The sight of her, carrying not just our child but the burden of our twisted situation, made my chest ache.

I watched as she set the table for dinner, her hands trembling slightly as she poured wine into two glasses—one for her, one for Naz. My heart sank as I saw her pull out the cologne bottle, carefully dripping a few drops into his glass. It felt like a nightmare in slow motion when Naz walked into the apartment and, upon seeing her, broke down in tears.

Hope stood by the table, her hand gently cradling her swollen belly. The soft glow of the kitchen light flickered across her face, illuminating a tender smile as she gestured to Naz, drawing his attention to her belly. She then handed him the glass of wine, her smile unwavering, as if this was just another ordinary evening.

Disgust twisted in my gut as I watched Naz kiss Hope's belly, then leap to his feet to plant a sloppy kiss on her lips. He lifted her off the ground and spun her around, laughing like they were in some twisted fairytale. Hope forced a smile and raised her glass, trying to propose a toast, but Naz gently took the glass from her hand, wagging his thieving fingers at her as if scolding a child.

Hope kept pressing, urging Naz to drink his wine. I saw her go to the freezer, return with ice, and drop it into his glass. Naz finally took a sip, but then paused, sniffing the wine suspiciously. His face twisted in anger, and he started arguing with Hope. The tension in the room exploded when he slammed the glass to the floor and slapped Hope hard across the face, sending her crashing to the ground. She landed with her belly right beside the shattered glass, her body curled in on itself as she tried to shield her stomach from the shards.

That was it! Fury ignited inside me, propelling me to my feet before I even realized it. I bolted towards the building, my heart pounding so fiercely it drowned out everything except the overwhelming urge to reach Hope.

I tore through the front doors, barreled past Sean without a word, demanding he call the police as I sprinted up the stairs two at a time. Each floor felt like an eternity, the distance between me and the seventh floor stretching impossibly long. The sounds of shouting and muffled struggle echoed down the stairwell as I neared the top.

Finally, I reached the seventh floor and slammed into the apartment door, bursting inside like a madman. There stood Hope, backed against the wall, her eyes wide with terror, and there was Naz—my own twisted reflection—towering over her. He was in a frenzy, slapping her, kicking at her legs, screaming right in front of her face.

"You trying to poison me?" he snarled, his hand raised to strike. "I know that sweaty cologne when I smell it. You could've killed me."

I didn't think—I just acted. In an instant, I was across the room, tackling Naz to the ground. Adrenaline surged through me as I threw him against the walls, lifted his body, and slammed him onto the floor. He was helpless, too weak and too scared to fight back, but I didn't care. I kept going, unleashing all my pent-up frustration and rage on him. I threw him, kicked him, punched him, then grabbed him by the neck and squeezed, feeling the life drain from his face beneath my grip.

"Go, Hope!" I shouted, keeping Naz pinned down by his neck. "Get out of here!"

But she didn't move. She sat there, leaning against the wall, holding her stomach, her cries filling the room as she watched in horror.

Hope needed me. My grip on Naz's neck loosened, reluctant as I was to let go. I scrambled to my feet, my heart pounding with urgency. Naz lay on the floor, a pitiful sight— crying, bleeding, and gasping for air, his face smeared with blood and tears. But I didn't spare him another glance. I rushed to Hope's side, her pale face etched with pain and fear. Blood pooled around Naz, staining the pristine floors of the condo, but all I could focus on was Hope—her trembling hands, her tear-streaked cheeks, and the life we were both desperately trying to protect.

"Help!" I called out. "Somebody, please..."

Hope was curled into the fetal position, her body trembling with each wave of pain. Half-conscious, she looked up at me, her eyes wide with fear and desperation. Her gaze shifted past me, locking onto something behind my back. I turned, catching sight of Naz crawling toward the kitchen, his movements sluggish and weak. His energy was nearly spent, but my priority was clear. I turned back to Hope, her pain-filled eyes grounding me in the moment, urging me to stay focused on her. Naz was a shadow, a fading threat. Hope was all that mattered.

"I'm sorry, baby," she whispered, her voice barely audible as a weary sob escaped her. "I just wanted to help... I couldn't have you risk your life..." Her words trailed off as she lost consciousness, collapsing into my arms.

Fear like I'd never known gripped me, icy and suffocating.

"No! Please don't die," I pleaded, my voice trembling as I cradled her limp body.

Ruth staggered into the condo, her movements unsteady as if the floor beneath her swayed like a ship at sea. She bumped into the doorframe, muttering under her breath, but her drunken haze couldn't fully mask the panic that flared in her eyes when she saw Hope lying on the floor.

With a half-stumble, half-sprint, she poured herself across the room, her steps erratic and her balance shaky. Her words slurred as she called out, "Hope! Oh my God, Hope!" She dropped to her knees beside her friend, her hands trembling as she reached out, tipsy but determined to help. The hallway behind her filled with the murmur of concerned neighbors, their faces blurred together in a mix of shock and confusion as they spilled out of their apartments, drawn by the commotion.

The clatter of the silverware drawer cut through the chaos like a jagged knife. The sharp metallic screech of the butcher knife being yanked free echoed in the room, jolting me from my focus on Hope. I turned, my heart pounding in my chest, and saw Naz, bloodied and battered, struggling to raise the knife with a shaky grip.

The sight of Hope's unconscious form on the floor was a knife to my soul, a wound that had torn through my being. Tears welled in my eyes as I whispered a shaky, "I'm sorry," to her.

With a roar that echoed my inner turmoil, I charged at Naz. The knife buried itself in my gut with a searing pain that was almost welcome. My hands, driven by a wild, uncontainable fury, grabbed him with a vice-like grip, lifting him off the ground despite the agony.

"You took everything from me," I snarled through gritted teeth, my voice a guttural growl of raw emotion. With a powerful heave, I hurled him towards the window. The glass shattered violently, sending shards flying in every direction. As Naz sailed through the broken pane, his scream was swallowed by the night, leaving a void where once there was a man who had destroyed so much.

I staggered my way to the window and peered over the edge, my vision swimming with horror. From seven floors up, the sight of Naz—my body—crumpled and twisted on the pavement below was more than I could bear. The grotesque tableau of broken limbs and blood sent a crazy wave of nausea through me. The realization that this mangled form was once mine was overwhelming. My stomach heaved, and I puked out the window directly on top of what used to be my body.

The distant wail of sirens grew louder, and I could see the flashing lights of police cars reflecting off nearby buildings. As the officers arrived, their frantic movements contrasted sharply with the chaos below. They rushed to Naz's broken form, their faces set with grim determination. I could hear their muffled voices and the clamor of their radios as they began to assess the scene.

"Fuck him!" I yelled down to the officers, my voice raw and hoarse from the emotional and physical strain. "We need a doctor up here! There's a pregnant woman who's badly hurt!"

A few officers, their faces etched with urgency, began ascending the stairs. The weight of the situation pressed down on me, every second feeling like an eternity as I waited for them to reach us. The reality of what had happened crashed over me in waves of guilt and dread, mingling with the overwhelming need to protect Hope, whose safety was now my only priority.

People were gathering outside, their faces masks of shock and morbid curiosity as they stared at the crumpled figure stuck on the pavement. The body, lifeless and twisted in unnatural angles, was all that was left of the man. I should have felt something—grief, guilt, maybe even relief—but all I felt was numb. The distant echo of my heartbeat barely registered over the cacophony of chaos, as if my mind had shut down to protect me from the crushing weight of reality. The flashing lights, the shouts of more first responders, it all blurred together, fading into the background as I stood in that window, lost in the space between memory and despair.

I didn't fight the cops when they cuffed me, they beat my ass anyway. I didn't know what to say, still in shock so I kept my mouth closed and accepted my fate. As they dragged me down the stairs, my mind was a fog of confusion and despair.

The cool night air hit me as we exited the building, a stark contrast to the stuffy, chaotic apartment we'd just left. That's when I saw her – Hope, being wheeled out on a stretcher, Ruth stumbling alongside, her face streaked with tears. The sight jolted me out of my stupor.

"Hope!" I called out, my voice cracking. "Is she okay? Please, somebody tell me!"

But my pleas were drowned out by the cacophony around us. The paramedics worked frantically, attaching tubes and monitors as they loaded Hope into the ambulance. Ruth climbed in after her, casting one last, unreadable glance in my direction before the doors slammed shut.

As the ambulance peeled away, its sirens wailing into the night, something inside me snapped. I began thrashing against the officers holding me, my desperation giving me a strength I didn't know I possessed.

"You're arresting the wrong man!" I shouted, my voice hoarse and ragged. "That's not me down there! I'm Walter Mosley! The real Walter Mosley!"

The officers shoved me into the back of a patrol car, but I wasn't done. I kicked at the driver's seat, my whole body trembling with adrenaline and fear.

"I'm claustrophobic!" I yelled, the words tumbling out in a frenzied rush. "You don't understand! There was a body swap! The cologne... it's cursed! Please, you have to believe me!"

Outside the car, I could see people pointing, some laughing at my outburst. The officers exchanged knowing glances, smirking as they compared my face to the wanted posters they held.

"We finally got him, boys," one of them said, initiating a round of high-fives and backslaps.

Through the crowd, I spotted a familiar face—the old man from the church, leaning on his broom. His eyes met mine, filled not with judgment or mockery, but with a deep, unsettling disappointment. It was like he could see right through me, past all the lies and confusion to the scared, lost kid I really was.

As the patrol car pulled away from the curb, I slumped back in my seat, the fight draining out of me. The city lights blurred past the window, each one a reminder of the life I'd just lost. Hope's fate unknown, my identity in shambles, and the truth so far beyond belief that no one would ever listen.

I closed my eyes, letting the tears I'd been holding back finally fall. In that moment, surrounded by the wreckage of my choices, I realized that some curses can't be broken – they can only be endured.

CHAPTER TWENTY THREE

The clock on the wall ticked in sync with my heartbeat, echoing in this cold, sterile prison. Five years had passed since that night on the rooftop—one thousand eight hundred and twenty-five days, each marked by a tick, each a reminder of loss, regret, and the passage of time. I perched on the edge of the bed, my reflection staring back at me from the small, scratched mirror, showing a face I hardly recognized. Naz's face, older now, lines etched deep with sorrow, but those eyes —they were mine, haunted by the weight of memories and a thousand unanswered questions.

The sharp scent of disinfectant filled the room, burning my nostrils, reminding me of exactly where I was. The shuffling feet and muffled voices drifting through the hallway formed a symphony, and Nurse Jenkins' voice broke through the noise as she passed by, her words laced with a cheerfulness that was as fake as the walls around me.

"How are we doing today, Walter?" she chirped, her bright smile clashing with the dull, gray surroundings.

I gave her the same answer I always did, a nod, a mumbled "fine," because what else was there to say?

The truth was, I was far from fine. The memories of that night replayed in my mind like a broken record. Hope's blood on my hands, Naz's twisted smile, the sound of sirens that arrived too late. And now, five years later, those memories had hardened into something darker, something I couldn't shake.

Nurse Jenkins handed me the small cup of pills, her eyes scanning my face for signs of anything out of the ordinary. I hid them under my tongue, the bitterness coating my mouth, and Jenkins never bothered to check.

Five years of therapy, of doctors poking and prodding at

my mind, trying to piece together what went wrong. But they didn't have the answers, and neither did I. All I had were the memories—of Hope, of Naz, of that night that changed everything. And no matter how much time passed, those memories would never let me go.

I could barely go an hour without my thoughts pulling me back to the trial. I could almost smell the polished wood of the courtroom as I took the stand, faces in the crowd blurring together into a sea of judgment.

I told them everything—the body swap, the curse, the rooftop. The truth spilled out like a confession, raw and unreal, but I owed that much to Hope. The jury's faces were etched with disbelief, horror, and when the judge's gavel came down, the sound reverberated like a death sentence.

"Not guilty by reason of insanity," he declared, sealing my fate and consigning me to this place of white walls and confusion.

They called it schizophrenia, a break from reality. But

reality was the curse that chained me here.

It was on one of these endless days that Margie Jackson approached my room with an unusual glint in her eye. "Walter, you have a visitor," she said, her voice neutral but her expression betraying a hint of curiosity.

My heart skipped a beat. A visitor? After all this time? Margie led me down the familiar corridor to the same room where I had once met Sage. I stepped inside, determined to present a better image than Sage had all those years ago.

As the door opened, my breath caught in my throat. "Ruth," I breathed, my heart racing. She was older, grayer, but unmistakably Ruth. Her eyes met mine, and a storm of emotions washed over me—anger, pity, resignation. For a second, I saw Hope beside her, that gentle smile, but then she was gone, leaving a raw ache in her place.

"Walter," Ruth said, her voice thick with unshed tears. "We need to talk."

Ruth sat across from me, hands clasped tightly on the

table between us, the silence hanging heavy with the weight of all that was unsaid. My fingers drummed nervously on my thigh, betraying the anxiety I tried to swallow.

"Hope..." I started, my voice breaking. "Is she...?"

Tears welled in Ruth's eyes, and in that moment, I knew. My world collapsed, the room spinning around me as I struggled to breathe.

"She's gone, Walter," Ruth whispered, each word slicing through me. "She didn't make it through the birth."

The words echoed, cruel and final. I gripped the edge of the table. A sob built in my chest, threatening to break me.

"The baby?" I managed to ask, my voice barely more than a whisper.

"A boy," Ruth said, a small, bittersweet smile breaking through her grief. "Strong. Healthy. Beautiful."

Relief and sorrow warred within me—a son. Hope's final gift to me, to the world.

"I've been raising him," Ruth continued, her voice soft but

firm. "These past five years have been hard, but that boy... he's something special. Just like his mama."

I closed my eyes, trying to picture him—a little boy with Hope's eyes, her smile. A child I'd never held, never seen. The weight of what I'd missed was suffocating.

"He's got your stubbornness," Ruth added, a hint of amusement creeping into her voice. "And Hope's curiosity. Always asking questions, always wanting to know more. He's very active."

Ruth paused, looked around the room, then leaned in closer. "He also get angry. He get angry all the time. Remind me of him."

"So you think...?" I couldn't finish the question.

"I don't know. He's also kind, Walter. So kind. He'll give away his last cookie to a friend without a second thought. That makes me think of only you and Hope."

A ghost of a smile tugged at my lips. "Sounds like a handful."

Ruth nodded, her expression softening. "He is. Cute little bastard."

My heart swelled with a mix of pride and pain. This beautiful boy, possibly half me, definitely half Hope, growing up without us. The injustice of it all was almost too much to bear.

"Why are you here, Ruth?" I asked, opening my eyes to meet her gaze, my voice trembling with the storm inside me.

She took a deep breath, straightening her shoulders. "He needs his father, Walter. I'm not as young as I used to be, and that boy... he's got a fire in him. A curiosity about the world, about where he came from. I can't give him those answers. But you can."

My heart raced—hope, fear, everything crashing together. A chance to be a father, to make things right. But the cold reality of my situation loomed over me. "I'm locked up in here, Ruth. They think I'm living with psychosis."

"Then prove them wrong," she said, her voice resolute.

"Fight this. Get better. Be the man that boy needs you to be."

The room got quiet while I gathered my thoughts, thinking of ways that I could fight it, nothing real solid coming to mind. Ruth was calm, half smiling as if she knew something I didn't. She revealed what she knew when she yelled out, "Okay! I'm ready."

I thought the signal meant that she was ready to leave, but she only sat there. Minutes later, as if on cue, the door opened, and a small figure appeared in the doorway, peeking around the corner with wide, curious eyes. My breath caught in my throat, my heart pounding so hard I thought it might burst.

"Come on in, sweetie," Ruth called softly. "There's someone I want you to meet."

He stepped into the room, and time seemed to stop. He was perfect—Hope's eyes, wide and full of curiosity, looked up at me. My smile, tentative but bright, lit up his little face. Tears welled in my eyes, spilling over before I could hold them back.

"Hi," he said, his voice confident and clear, as if he'd never even fallen, as if he'd never learned to crawl, but instead, stood up and walked. It all sent a tremor through me.

"Hello," I managed, my voice thick with emotion. "I'm... my name is Walter. What's your name?"

He tilted his head, studying me with an intensity that was all Hope. He looked to Ruth, as if asking permission. Once she gave him the nod, he slowly stepped forward. "My name is Walter too," he said. "Walter Marshall Mosley."

I looked at Ruth; she was smiling ear to ear. "I didn't know any other famous authors, so I did the best I could."

Walter wrapped his arms around me. The feel of his small body against mine, the scent of innocence and new beginnings, shattered all the toughness inside me.

I hugged him back, careful, almost afraid that if I held him too tight, he might vanish like a dream. Tears flowed freely.

"I'm sorry," I whispered into his hair. "I'm so sorry I haven't been there. But I promise you, I'm going to do better. I'm going to be here for you."

As I held my son, breathing in the scent of all that was still possible, I felt something I hadn't felt in years—hope. And with that hope came a fierce determination. I would get better. I would fight this curse, this diagnosis, this madness. I would be the father this boy deserved.

For Hope. For our son. For the life we should have had.

As I bring this statement to a close, I'm struck by the weight of the journey that has brought me here. Five years ago, I entered these walls a man shattered by a reality that defied logic, bound by curses that twisted the very essence of who I was. I couldn't see a way out. But today, I'm writing to you not as that man, but as someone who has clawed his way out of darkness, faced the ghosts of his past, and is now ready to embrace a future with a clear purpose.

I know the story that led me here sounds like fiction—body swaps, mystical curses, a cologne that ensnares the soul—it's the stuff of legends, not life. I no longer seek your belief in these strange events. Instead, I ask that you see the man standing before you now. A man shaped by the extraordinary but defined by his response to it.

These five years have been a crucible, forcing me to confront the deepest parts of myself. I've learned that true strength doesn't come from running away, but from standing firm in the face of fear, from acknowledging every scar and imperfection. I've wrestled with my demons, processed the pain, and come to terms with the irreversible consequences of my past actions. Hope is gone, lost to a fate I'll always regret, and my original body is out of reach. These truths are as heavy as they are unchangeable, but they also remind me of the price of my missteps.

But even in the midst of this loss, I find hope—hope in my son, Walter Marshall Mosley. At five years old, he is my beacon, my reason for being. He's a future I once believed was out of my grasp, and he deserves a father who's more than a shadow, more than a memory of mistakes. He deserves a man who's present, a man who can teach him the hard-learned lessons of life, a man who can show him what it means to grow, to endure, and to love fiercely.

I am committed to my mental health treatments, to staying vigilant about my mental health, and to doing the work necessary to be the best version of myself. I'm not asking you to release a man who is "cured," but a man who is prepared to manage himself and contribute meaningfully to the world around him.

To Hope, wherever her spirit may rest, I vow to honor her by being the father our son deserves. To little Walter, I pledge to make up for every lost moment, to guide him with a steady hand, to love him with all the strength I have left, and to shape him into a man of honor and compassion.

But, I can only do that outside of this place.

I stand before you today, no longer the Walter Mosley who entered these halls, but a man reborn through fire, a man ready to live, to give, and to love with all that he is. I ask for the chance to step back into the world—not as a perfect man, but as a man committed to being better. A man ready to build a future, not just for himself, but for his son, and for the memory of the woman who gave him life.

Thank you for your consideration. I await your decision with hope, humility, and the determination to prove I am worthy of this second chance.

Respectfully submitted,

Walter Mosley

Patient #3324D

University of Chicago Hospital for Mental Health

Made in the USA
Middletown, DE
30 August 2024

60010464R00187